LITTLE ISAAC'S AMISH NANNY

AN AMISH ROMANCE

NAOMI TROYER

UNACCEPTABLE EXPECTATIONS

"*A*ch, Joseph, isn't it just a beautiful day? I'm so glad that winter is finally gone. I hate the cold." Beth Stoltzfus turned to Joseph with a beaming smile.

Joseph Yoder couldn't help but smile at his sweetheart. For the last two years he had been courting Beth and could pride himself on knowing most of her whims and likes and dislikes. He cocked a brow with a questioning look in his eyes. "Only until summer starts, Beth, then you hate the heat."

Beth playfully punched his arm. "You know me too well."

"So I do." Joseph smiled before he turned his gaze back on the road.

Beth's beauty never failed to amaze him. She had skin that appeared as soft as whipped cream and as light as cream as well. Her naturally auburn hair shone copper when the sun caught a strand peeking out from her prayer kapp. And then of course there were her eyes. Beth had been blessed with the most unique shade of green eyes Joseph had ever seen. It was a mix between freshly cut grass and emeralds, changing hues depending on her mood.

Joseph couldn't help but feel privileged she had accepted his invitation for a buggy ride two years ago. Many young men in the community had been disappointed when they learned that he and Beth had gone steady.

He had taken a different route today, one he hadn't driven with Beth in a very long time.

After the news he received this morning, Joseph needed the distraction. In the distance he could see the trees budding with new leaves. It was as if the entire world came back to life after a long and cold winter. Bird song hung in the air as Beth chattered on. Not that Joseph was trying to ignore her, he just had too much on his mind. The last thing that concerned him now was the new rug Beth's mother had purchased for their living room.

"Joseph! Are you listening to me?" Beth asked suddenly, turning to him with a petulant look.

Joseph shrugged and smiled apologetically. "I'm sorry, sweetheart. I'm just a little distracted today. I still can't believe Mrs. Brahms has passed away. Two days ago, I saw her. When I was there on Thursday, she looked healthy as can be."

"Are you really telling me you're thinking about a dead widow while we're on our weekly buggy ride?" Beth demanded with anger in her gaze.

"Holy heavens Beth, show a little respect," Joseph demanded with an exasperated look.

"What? She was like a hundred years old, people die when they get old, it's the way of life." Beth shrugged as if Mrs. Brahms' death didn't matter to her at all.

Joseph drew in a deep breath and reminded himself that Beth wouldn't understand. She had lost no one close to her. Whereas Joseph had too much experience in that department. One year ago he'd been taking care of his four-year-old brother Isaac while his parents went to visit family in Ohio.

It was supposed to be just a week of watching after his brother, instead it had turned into a lifetime commitment.

When the bishop relayed the news of the passing of his

parents, Joseph had been dumbstruck. While mourning the loss of his parents, he became guardian to a four-year-old at twenty-three.

The bus on which they had been travelling had been in an accident on the highway on its way back to Lancaster County. There had been five fatalities, which included Joseph's parents. Joseph knew what it was like to stand beside the grave of someone you loved. Joseph understood what it felt like to miss someone so badly that your heart ached.

Of course Mrs. Brahms hadn't been family, but she had been his brother's caretaker for the last year. Just like Isaac had grown fond of Mrs. Brahms, Joseph cared for her as well. For five days a week she had watched his brother, fed him, and nursed his childhood wounds. Isaac was grieving more than Joseph for the widow, but Joseph now found himself in a terrible bind.

Without Mrs. Brahms to look after Isaac, he had no childcare in place. As a crop farmer, Joseph simply couldn't watch after Isaac all day.

Of course there was Mrs. Leipoldt in town who watched a few of the Amish children during the week, but Joseph didn't want to consider that as an option. Isaac had already lost his parents and now he lost the person who he adored as a second mother or a grandmother figure.

Sending Isaac to an Englischer for daycare simply wasn't an option. Joseph needed to take care of his brother, needed to assure his brother that he wasn't going away.

Because after losing so many loved ones, Isaac had asked him this morning why everyone goes *away*.

It had nearly torn Joseph's heart in two to hear his brother ask a question like that at his tender age. Isaac needed love and attention. He needed to know that he was loved, cherished, and that he was safe. Sending him to a daycare facility now, especially with unfamiliar people, would only make matters more difficult for his brother.

Joseph finally let out a heavy sigh before he spoke. "Seventy-three to be exact."

"Exactly," Beth scoffed. "That's *old!*"

"Regardless, she was kind and caring, especially to Isaac," Joseph pointed out. "With her gone, I do not know what I'm going to do," Joseph admitted.

"Send him to daycare, everyone does," Beth suggested as if she had just suggested he buy his brother an ice-cream to get over his grief.

"Nee, that simply isn't an option," Joseph said simply.

"Then what about your neighbor, Mrs. Schwartz? She doesn't mind watching him when we go on buggy rides," Beth suggested.

Joseph shook his head. "I considered asking Mrs. Schwartz, but she told me at the funeral this morning that she just accepted a position at the farm stall."

"Then daycare is the only other option," Beth shrugged as if it settled the matter.

Joseph frowned. "Beth, I can't send him to daycare. He needs to be close to me, close to familye. He's already lost too much at his young age." An idea formed in Joseph's mind as he searched Beth's green gaze. "What about you?"

Beth's eyes widened with surprise before they widened even more with horror. "Are you kidding?"

"Nee," Joseph shook his head as hope swelled in his chest. "We're courting, Beth, and you have the free time. Surely you understand how much it will mean to me if you could help. Isaac would be right there on the farm with me, he wouldn't have to leave every day... It's the perfect solution Beth, it's what Isaac needs."

Beth's family were the wealthiest in the community. Except for a few chores around the house, Beth had never worked a day in her life. Joseph didn't think of her as spoiled, but as privileged. Now he couldn't help but hope that his sweetheart would use her privileges in life to bless him with a little kindness.

Beth shook her head defiantly. "Joseph, I adore you, you know I do. It was devastating to see you grieve after you lost your parents and I know how hard it was for you to take over your brother's care. But this... Joseph, I have no interest in spending all my free time with a little boy. I'm sorry if this sounds a little harsh, but Isaac is your problem, not mine."

Her refusal did not too surprise Joseph, but he was a little shocked at her choice of words. Knowing that Beth wasn't the solution, Joseph changed the subject hoping to salvage what was left of their buggy ride.

THE PERFECT POSITION

*H*ope Maas glanced down at her plate at the dinner table and couldn't help but feel guilty. At nineteen she should be able to contribute to the family's income, and yet after a year of trying to find a job, she still had had no luck.

Although her parents, Abram and Ruth, insisted they managed whenever Hope brought up the subject, she knew they were just being kind. As the eldest of five children, Hope couldn't help but feel as if she was becoming a burden to her parents. With seven mouths to feed three times a day, the income from the farm was far away from making ends meet.

Hope was the oldest at nineteen, then Peter followed at the age of seventeen. After Peter her parents had been blessed with another girl, Louisa. Louisa was only eleven years old now. Then there was Daniel who had just turned eight a month before and last, but not least, was everyone's favorite: Rose.

Rose had been a very unexpected addition to their family. With fifteen years age difference between Hope and her youngest sister, she had been very involved with Rose's care since the day she was born.

Their house was one that was always filled with love, laughter, and joy–regardless of the shortcomings they might have. If Hope had to list the shortcomings they had tonight, the list would be very long, starting with a new pair of shoes and a pair of pants for Peter who was growing faster than weeds could infiltrate their crops.

Louisa's dresses had all been passed down from Hope but were fading and no longer looked appealing at all. Then there was Daniel's coat that was much too small and her mother who refused to buy herself a new apron after hers was stained.

They might not be wealthy in earthly riches, but just glancing around the table, Hope knew her family was rich with riches of the heart.

Her father was a fifth-generation crop farmer; he always had a variety of vegetable crops growing in the fields. Ever since Hope had finished her education in the Amish schoolhouse, she had been helping her parents at home and around the farm.

Peter had also worked on the farm when he finished school and was now working by her father's side every day. One day Peter would inherit the family farm, and he was determined to learn everything he could from their father.

With Peter helping in the fields and Louisa helping with Rose and the chores around the house, it was time for Hope find employment outside the home. Employment that would benefit her family financially.

In the last year alone, she had applied at almost every farm stall, grocer, retail outlet, and coffeeshop in their small town. Either she wasn't qualified according to Englisch standards, or they simply didn't want an Amish person on their payroll. Hope wouldn't ever know which it was.

As everyone took their seats at the dinner table, Hope already knew that tonight she would pray once more for Gott to bless her with a job. One that she could enjoy, and even if she didn't enjoy it, one that would help ease her parents' financial burdens.

"The food looks nutritious and delicious," Abram Maas said as he took a seat at the head of the table.

Hope smiled, her father said that every single night before they said their prayers.

"It's just a stew, Abram, don't get too excited." Ruth Maas smiled at her husband from across the table.

Hope didn't mind stew at all, but she had noticed that it had become a staple in their home. With money being tight as it was, her mother stretched ingredients much further with stews than other dishes.

"Let us pray."

Everyone bowed their heads in silent prayer, even Rose knew it was time to respect the Lord and to thank him for the blessings on the table.

After a moment's silence everyone began serving themselves.

"I weeded the tomatoes today, Daed. Hopefully, they won't return," Peter said before taking a bite of his food.

"That's gut. Every drop of water a weed drinks, is a drop of water another plant loses," her father commented wisely.

"Did you enjoy your prayer group, my mann?" Ruth asked.

Every week, ever since Hope could remember, her father joined the prayer group for men. As a deacon, many people in the community relied on her father's wisdom and prayers.

"Jah. It humbles me every week to know how blessed our familye is to have each other. There are some members of the congregation that are truly suffering from the actions of their familye. I learned again today that to respond in anger is never a solution."

Hope listened as her father spoke. Her father would never reveal whom he had prayed for, but some weeks more than others, Hope could see that the problems of the community weighed heavy on her father's shoulders.

"We are truly blessed," Ruth agreed with a nod.

Her father's face suddenly lit up, as if he had completely

forgotten to share something with them. "Even more blessed today than yesterday."

"Abram?" her mother asked, confused.

"After the prayer meeting, the bishop called me aside. He found a job for Hope."

Hope's eyes lit up even as excitement washed over her. "He did? Where?"

"It's perfect, Hope," her father began. "You'll be a nanny to a five-year-old boy. Your duties will include caring for him during the week from eight o'clock until five in the afternoon. Cleaning isn't expected but will be appreciated."

Her father continued to explain what the wages would be and what other duties would be expected of her, such as stimulating the boy's curious mind. It sounded almost too good to be true. The more Hope listened, the more excited she became.

Being the eldest of five children and helping her mother raise her siblings, she loved children. She loved their curious minds, their eagerness to learn, and more than anything, she enjoyed caring for them. It made her feel appreciated, as if she was making a difference in someone's life.

When her father was finished, a frown creased Hope's brow. There had to be a catch. "Is it for Englischers, Daed?"

Her father shook his head. "Nee. It for someone in our own community. Mrs. Brahms, who passed away last week, used to care for the boy before she passed on."

Hope's eyes widened with fear. "I'll be working for Joseph Yoder?"

"Ach gut, you know him," her father said, pleased.

"Daed, I..." Hope tried to find a reason that she couldn't work for Joseph Yoder but couldn't think of a single valid reason. Telling her father that she felt intimidated by the tall man with piercing blue eyes wouldn't be acceptable.

"Hope, to find work is a blessing, remember that," her mother reminded her firmly.

Hope nodded. "Of course it is, I'm very grateful. When do I start?"

"Tomorrow," her father smiled at her from across the table. "The boy's name is Isaac. He is Joseph's younger bruder."

"Wait," Hope frowned as she puzzled the pieces together. "Joseph became guardian to Isaac when they lost their parents last year, jah?"

"Jah," her father confirmed.

Regardless of being slightly terrified of Joseph Yoder, Hope decided there and then that she would do her very best to care for Isaac. She couldn't imagine how hard it must have been for him to lose his parents at such a young age.

"I'll do right by him, Daed. Denke for arranging it," Hope finally said.

"I know you will, no one is more suited to care for a little boy than you, Hope. You could do it in your sleep and still you'd enjoy it," Ruth smiled at her daughter.

Hope returned her mother's smile knowing her mother was right. Being a nanny to a little boy wouldn't feel like work at all, it would be a privilege.

THE CHICKEN IS OUT OF THE NEST

"Come cluckies, come!" Isaac called as Joseph opened the gate of the chicken coop. He allowed Isaac to walk in ahead of him, knowing feeding the chickens was the highlight of his brother's day.

Joseph had been raised the Amish way and knew his parents would've wanted him to raise his brother the same. Although there were many cultures in the world that didn't believe in giving children work or responsibility, the Amish believed differently.

The Amish believed chores were one of the most fundamental lessons of life. It not only taught you to respect the work others do around the house and the yard but teaches you about the responsibility to contribute. From a very young age, they had given Joseph chores around the house, and he carried on that tradition with Isaac.

At first it had been small things like putting your toys away and putting dirty clothes in the laundry hamper. From there more chores were added every year. Now, Isaac's latest chore was to take care of the chickens.

Giving children chores they enjoyed not only instilled a good work ethic in them, but it ceased complaining about the work.

Joseph always supervised Isaac, to make sure that both Isaac and the chickens survived every feed.

"Cluckies, come and get it!" Isaac cried out with excitement as he tossed a handful of chicken feed into the air.

The chickens flapped their wings and scurried to the ground, pecking up every morsel of food, making Isaac giggle with joy. The process was repeated ten times before the feeding was done. Next, Joseph helped Isaac fill their water bowl with fresh water from the bucket they had filled before coming into the coop.

Although Joseph was very present in the entire process, he couldn't help but feel a little anxious this morning. At Sunday service he had mentioned his childcare problem to the bishop. The bishop had promised to help him find a solution.

Joseph had thought the bishop would try to convince Joseph to send Isaac to the daycare center in town. But he sent word yesterday that he had found the perfect candidate to be Isaac's nanny.

The new nanny was to start this morning and although Joseph was grateful for the help, he couldn't help but feel a little anxious. Isaac was the most important person in Joseph's life and the last thing he wanted was to leave Isaac in the care of someone that was too stern or didn't care for children at all.

In Joseph's mind the perfect nanny for his brother was someone who was a little further along in age, someone like Mrs. Brahms. Someone who would be patient enough to listen to Isaac's imaginative tales and yet firm enough to discipline him in a kind way.

Since the housekeeping chores had fallen onto the back-burner since his parents passed away, he hoped the nanny might be able to help him in that department as well. He didn't expect the new nanny to spring clean the house every day, or even do the dishes, but merely to assist with the chores that he didn't get to.

"There, all done!" Isaac smiled up at Joseph with a wide grin. "Is she here yet?"

Joseph shook his head. "Soon, bruder. Let's go get you breakfast, then we'll wait for her on the porch."

Isaac nodded obediently. Joseph had taken care to explain to Isaac last night that although he enjoyed his company and wouldn't mind playing with him all day, he had to work as well. He had told Isaac about a new nanny that would look after him at home, just like Mrs. Brahms did, but this time he wouldn't have to go to her house.

Unlike Joseph, Isaac seemed excited, not anxious in the least.

After a sturdy breakfast of oats and a banana, Joseph made himself a cup of coffee before he went to wait for the new nanny out on the porch. It was ten to eight, which meant she would be arriving soon.

Isaac seemed just as relieved as Beth that winter was finally over. He celebrated every minute he could spend playing outdoors after being kept inside over the winter. After barely a few minutes, Isaac had thought up a game which involved running from the one side of the front yard to the other before jumping onto the bottom step of the porch and jumping off again.

Joseph wished he had his little brother's endless energy sometimes. He watched as Isaac did another circuit before he heard a soft voice beside the porch.

"Hullo?"

Joseph's brow furrowed at the sight of the young girl. He stood up; certain she was lost. "Hullo?"

She seemed vaguely familiar, but he couldn't immediately place her. Their community was one of the largest in Lancaster County. It was impossible for him to know every single person that was part of their congregation.

"I… uhm… I'm Beth Stoltzfus. The bishop said you needed a nanny?"

Joseph's gaze travelled over the young girl. She couldn't be a day over fifteen, he reasoned. Her hair was a light brown shade, with touches of honey in her fringe. Her prayer kapp was neatly tied over her head, her dress and apron perfectly ironed, albeit a little faded with age.

She had a sharp chin and a petulant nose. Her eyes weren't the usual shade of brown, rather a light shade of hazel, and right now those hazel eyes were waiting for him to respond.

"The bishop sent you?" Joseph could hear the disillusion in his own voice.

"Jah." She nodded before glancing at Isaac who was doing another circuit of his imaginary game.

Joseph couldn't be sure what the bishop had been thinking, but he knew without doubt that this girl was too young to care for Isaac. Aside from being a child herself, she seemed much too timid to handle a busy five-year-old boy.

And she was nothing like Mrs. Brahms. She wasn't old, she wasn't wrinkled, and she wasn't comfortably set.

Instead, she glowed with youth.

"I'm sorry," Joseph began, coming down from the porch to meet her. "I think the bishop misunderstood me. Denke for coming all this way, but your services won't be required."

Hope jutted out her chin stubbornly. "What did the bishop misunderstand? You're in need of childcare, jah?"

"Jah, but from someone with a little experience. Not someone who had been in diapers only a few years ago. Like I said, I apologize for your trouble, but I simply cannot entrust a child to another child." Joseph's voice was firm. He wasn't about to argue with a child. At the end of the day, Isaac was his responsibility, and he was going to do what he thought was best for his brother.

And that was not this dewy looking teenager.

MAGIC POTIONS TO THE RESCUE

Hope crossed her arms even as her eyes narrowed. She had only seen Joseph Yoder from afar and his tall frame and crystal blue eyes had always intimidated her. If the situation had been different, she would've turned on her heel and headed back home.

But her family needed the money, and she needed the work.

She was about to explain to Joseph Yoder, imposing as he might seem, that she wasn't a child and that she was perfectly capable of caring for a five-year-old when suddenly a cry of pain caught her attention.

Hope saw the little boy lying beside the porch step and began to run without even thinking. She didn't wait for Joseph's permission or approval, she just jumped into action like she usually did when one of her siblings got hurt.

"Hullo, my name is Hope," Hope explained calmly as she kneeled beside the crying boy. "Tell me where it hurts."

The little boy's face was scrunched up with pain, tears staining his cheeks. He held onto his right foot, sobbing as he tried to explain. "Foot, my foot hurts."

Hope nodded. "I can see that. What's your name, honey?"

"Isaac," Joseph's deep voice answered behind her.

Only then did Hope realize he was standing to one side, flustered by the situation.

"Alright, Isaac. Can I look at your foot? I promise I won't hurt it more." When Isaac nodded, Hope carefully reached for the foot he had been holding.

Isaac's eyes were wide with fear as Hope gently slid her hands over the arch of his foot, his toes, and finally his ankle. "Can you move it?"

Isaac's foot moved, but when Isaac cried out with pain, Hope realized the slight movement caused him discomfort. Having seen this type of injury numerous times with her siblings, she didn't even have to second guess the problem.

"That's very gut. It's just a sprain, but it still hurts, doesn't it?" Hope asked as she began to slip one arm beneath his shoulders and the other beneath his knees. "We'll put some ice on it and then we'll wrap it in a bandage. Two or three sleeps and you won't even remember it was hurt," Hope promised as she scooped him up and stood up straight.

Isaac snuggled into her shoulder, still sobbing quietly.

Hope turned to Joseph with a questioning look. "Kitchen?"

"This way." Joseph led her into the kitchen and once again seemed a little lost with how to handle the situation. Realizing he would need instructions, Hope gave them. "I need ice, a bandage, and tea."

Joseph nodded and began to move. He returned a few moments later with ice before he left again.

Hope wrapped the ice in a dish cloth before she iced Isaac's ankle. "If it was winter, we could've just stuck it in the snow, but this will work."

"Does snow fix things?" Isaac asked, distracted by her comment, exactly what Hope had hoped for.

"Jah. Didn't you know it has healing magic? Whenever you get a hurt like this one, and you put ice or snow on it, it gets better much faster."

Joseph returned and set a bandage on the table before he moved to the wood stove where he began to brew a pot of tea.

"There, how does that feel?" Hope asked Isaac.

"It doesn't hurt so much anymore." Isaac sniffed again.

"Gut, because now I'm going to rub on a magic potion." Hope winked at Isaac before she reached into her purse that was still hanging on her shoulder. She pulled out a small jar and wriggled it in the air. "This is a magic potion I brew myself; it will take the pain away just like summer chases winter away."

Hope noticed Joseph's confused look from the stove. As she opened the jar and took a little bit out, she explained. "Don't fret, it's just turmeric, water, lemon juice, and a few drops of arnica oil. It helps with aches and sprains."

She rubbed the balm between her hands until it was nice and warm before she began applying it to Isaac's now ice-cold ankle. She gently rubbed the ankle until it was warm to her touch before she reached for the bandage. Once the ankle was wrapped with the bandage, she clapped her hands together. "There you go, all fixed up. You can leave that on for two sleeps and when you take it off, your foot will be ready to jump on the porch steps again."

"And the tea?" Joseph asked, holding up the fresh pot of tea.

"Pour him a cup with extra sugar and cream, he deserves it." Hope stood up and gathered her purse before turning to Isaac. "It was nice to meet you, Isaac."

Without even saying goodbye to Joseph, she turned and walked out of the kitchen. She wouldn't beg him for the position. She knew she was capable and if Joseph didn't think that, then it was his loss.

Although she really did need the money…

She was halfway down the porch when she heard his footsteps rushing in her direction.

"Hope, wait," Joseph called after her.

Hope drew in a deep breath before she turned and met his gaze with a questioning look. "Jah?"

"How old are you?" Joseph asked with a confused expression.

"I'm nineteen, and far from just a child," Hope snapped irritably. If this child hadn't been there, she would've loved to see how Joseph had dealt with a sprained ankle.

Joseph's brow furrowed even more. "But you don't look a day over fourteen…" He shook his head as if to gather his thoughts. "I'm sorry, what I meant was, I thought you were much younger. What you just did, how you handled the situation… denke."

"I have four younger bruders and schweschders, I'm used to being around kinner and injuries. It's part of growing up." Hope shrugged. "I hope you find the right nanny for him; he seems like a great little boy."

Hope was about to leave again when Joseph took another step closer. "I apologize for the way I acted before." He dragged a hand through his brown hair, his crystal blue eyes searching hers. "I just want to do what's right for my bruder and sometimes it's hard to know what that is."

Hope smiled for the first time since meeting Joseph officially. "He's blessed to have you looking out for him."

"Can we please start over? I'd love to hire you as Isaac's nanny," Joseph said with a hopeful look.

"I'd love to take care of Isaac. And although I'm not saying that I'm right for him, I can promise you I will always try and do the right thing for him… and for you," Hope promised softly.

Joseph smiled and held out his hand. "Can you start tomorrow? I think we've had enough excitement for one day."

Laughter bubbled from Hope's throat. "I'll be here first thing. Keep that ankle elevated, it will prevent swelling."

They shook hands before Hope headed home, eager to tell her parents the good news.

Finally, she was gainfully employed. Although she didn't feel her employer was very approachable, she already adored Isaac.

BEHIND ENEMY LINES

oseph had spent the last few days plowing through the winter-hardened fields. In a month he would begin to sow his corn, but for now, tilling and fertilizing the land was paramount to a good crop.

His draught horse had worked just as hard as he had and was also huffing when they reached the end of the field they had been plowing. Joseph stood for a moment to catch his breath, and as was habit his gaze travelled to his home in the distance.

From where he stood, he could see the old red barn, the house, and the laundry line. The chicken coop obscured most of the yard between the barn and the house, but he could still see the front yard. Every time he saw Isaac in the yard, he had a moment of panic before he realized Hope was there to look after him.

Hope.

Joseph let out a quiet sigh and wondered how long it would take to get used to having her around. It still felt strange to walk into the kitchen and to find her cooking at the stove, or to see her sweeping the porch.

Clearly, Isaac didn't have that problem at all. Isaac had taken to Hope's presence as if it had been a blessing gifted to him by Gott. He adored his new nanny and kept chattering on about her hours after she left in the evenings.

Joseph couldn't really blame his brother at all. Besides being young, Hope was a kind and caring young woman who adored his brother just as much as he did.

As he stood and watched the house, he noticed Hope sitting beside the laundry line. At her feet was the large tub Joseph used to wash the laundry in. She looked up and laughed at Isaac before she continued to run an item over the washing board.

Joseph shook his head, baffled by her capabilities. When he had hired her, he had hoped she might find the time to cook every now and then, perhaps help with a little light cleaning when Isaac was napping. Instead, she had completely blown him away by taking over his entire household, in a good way.

In the week she had been taking care of Isaac, she had washed the curtains and the linens, scrubbed the floors, and cleaned the pantry. She had also somehow found the time to cook them dinner every night and sweep the house every single day.

It was much more than Joseph expected of her. When he'd told her that, she had simply explained that she enjoyed keeping busy and that taking care of Isaac wasn't taxing at all.

Unlike with Joseph, Isaac seemed to obey Hope's every request. If she asked him to stay in the yard, he did so without question.

A week after the fact, Joseph could finally admit that the bishop had been right, Hope had been the perfect choice as a nanny for his young brother.

Having caught his breath, he moved towards the horse and began to plow in the other direction. The afternoon light faded as he worked, thoughts of Hope and her efforts remaining firmly on his mind. By the time he had fed and watered the horse and finished with the evening chores, he was exhausted and as hungry as a lion who hadn't eaten in a month.

The scent caught him even before he opened the back door.

Joseph stepped into the kitchen and smiled at the sight of meatloaf on the table. "You cooked that?"

"Jah, I thought you might be tired of stews and pasta," Hope explained as she carried green beans and a separate bowl of baby carrots to the table.

"This looks delicious, but you know you don't have to cook every night?" Joseph advised her again.

Hope shrugged. "I enjoy cooking, I really don't mind."

Joseph glanced around the kitchen and couldn't spot his brother. "Where is Isaac?"

"He's just had his bath. He's putting away his dirty clothes and cleaning up the bathroom. He'll be here soon," Hope said with a smile over her shoulder. "If there is anything specific, you'd like me to cook, I'd be happy to try."

Joseph frowned at the woman in front of him. Did she even realize what a help she has been? And now to offer to cook him special meals as well? "You really don't have to… did you wash the windows?" Joseph moved into the living room and noticed the windows in there were also crystal clear.

"Jah," Hope laughed softly. "Isaac had a wunderbaar time. We even had a soap sud fight."

"He helped?" Joseph asked, baffled.

"I wouldn't say help, but he tried very hard to help." Hope smiled affectionately. "He's really eager to help and to learn."

"Jah he is…" Joseph trailed off. How was it that Hope seemed to manage more in day whilst caring for his brother than he did in a week? "I can barely manage to get anything done when I have to take care of him," Joseph admitted.

He expected Hope to laugh or to tease him, but instead she smiled at him with kindness in her eyes. "I've had a lot of practice so don't be too hard on yourself."

"Joseph! Did you see the windows?" Isaac asked a moment

later. He blew into the kitchen with the energy of a summer tornado.

Joseph turned to the window before meeting his brother's gaze. "Where are the windows? Did you break them all?"

Isaac's giggles filled the air. "They're still there silly, they've just been washed."

"So have you," Joseph said, smiling at his brother. "Did you enjoy your bath?"

Isaac nodded. "We had to cross *enemeney* lines. We asked the dirt and germs to jump off, but they wouldn't listen." Isaac glanced at Hope with a serious expression. "She had to bring out the soap."

Joseph couldn't help but laugh. It seemed Hope's imagination was just as vividly wild as his brother's. "I'm glad to see the soap got the upper hand."

"Dinner is on the table, enjoy your evening," Hope said with her purse over her shoulder.

Something twinged inside Joseph, regretting that it was time for her to leave. He met her gaze with a bold smile, gratitude in his gaze. "Denke, Hope. Not just for the food, or the bath, or the windows… but for everything. I appreciate it, all of it, more than I can say."

She smiled shyly at him. "It's my pleasure."

For a moment Joseph couldn't look away, it was Hope who broke their gazes. She turned to Isaac and cocked a firm brow. "Now remember to say your prayers and to brush those teeth before bed. You don't want the army of germs to win the last battle of the day."

Isaac laughed at her words. "Night Hope."

Joseph walked her to the door and watched her leave. Before he returned to join his brother at the dinner table he glanced up at the sky and thanked the Lord for sending Hope to help him care for his brother.

He had hoped that Beth would be up to the task, especially since they were courting, but now he knew that it had to be Hope. After everything his brother had lost, Hope was a wonderful addition to his life. Pleased with his decision to hire her, Joseph headed towards the kitchen, eager to spend some time with his brother.

UNEXPECTED CHARM

As Hope walked home in the fading light of the afternoon, she couldn't stop thinking about Joseph. The way he had looked at her had made something twist inside her, something that had never felt before. And when he smiled at her…

The twisting sensation in her tummy had doubled, no tripled, before it made her head spin and her knees quiver beneath her weight. It hadn't been his usual 'thank you' smile. Instead, it had been much more powerful.

It was as if he had captured her gaze, holding her prisoner in the moment, with no way to escape. Hope had never experienced anything like it before in her entire life. Of course, she had been thanked by people numerous times in her life, but this was the first time a simple thank you had made her feel more appreciated and important than she had ever felt before.

For Hope, cooking, cleaning, and watching children had always been part of her life. She appreciated Joseph's gratitude, but she honestly didn't feel as if she was going out of her way to do more than what was necessary.

Her mother had taught her from a very young age that if

certain tasks were left for too long, they became harder to complete. If you regularly scrubbed your floors, an intensive scrubbing wouldn't ever be necessary. Just like if you did the laundry twice a week, you wouldn't have to spend a whole day dedicated to only laundry the following week.

Hope had never realized how much she had learned from her mother. Until now, she had only helped around the house and did things the way she had been taught, but now she was grateful for everything she had learned at home.

Hope shook her head and tried to shake off the feeling, but it was close to impossible. It was if her mind wouldn't stop spinning, and the image of Joseph smiling at her had been burned into her memory.

She was almost halfway home when she realized what the twisting sensation had been... attraction. Hope had heard her friends describe the feeling, but she had never experienced it for herself. There had been boys she had gotten along with at school, but not once had one of them captured her attention in the way that Joseph had.

Up until today she had been careful, almost distant towards him. After their tumultuous introduction, she had thought that he despised her. That he only kept her on for Isaac's sake. She hadn't talked to him unless it was necessary and always left the moment he returned from the fields.

But today, Joseph hadn't been imposing at all.

He had been... friendly, charming, almost.

The sudden change in his behavior towards her had thrown Hope off kilter. It had been as unexpected as worms in a chicken coop.

Her heart skipped a beat as she thought of his smile again. Perhaps she had misjudged Joseph Yoder. Perhaps he wasn't the rude, imposing, and quiet man she had thought him to be. Perhaps he was charming, kind, and friendly.

Knowing that her handsome employer could be kind and

courteous made her a little more wary of him. She couldn't help but be afraid that if she had felt that twist once, that it would happen again. And if it did...

Hope pushed the thoughts aside, thoughts that made her mind travel in a direction they had never travelled before.

Courtship.

As soon as the thought occurred to her, she gasped with surprise. She had no right to even think of courtship and Joseph Yoder in the same sentence. He was at least six years older than her, if she remembered correctly from when they were at school, and then, of course, there was Beth Stoltzfus.

Everyone in the community knew of the Stoltzfus family. Not only were they the wealthiest family around but also known to everyone through their involvement with all community events.

It was no secret to Hope that Beth and Joseph had been courting for the last two years. Just a few months ago, Hope's friends discussed how their engagement would be delayed due to Joseph losing his parents.

Hope arrived home and vowed before entering the house that she would steel herself against the effect Joseph had had on her. He had a sweetheart, and she had no business feeling attracted to him. The only reason she saw him was because he hired her to take care of Isaac.

A smile curved on Hope's mouth as she walked into the living room and set down her purse. In just a week, Isaac had won her over. His curiosity, adorable smile, and kind eyes had already crawled into her heart.

"There you are," Hope's mother said when Hope walked into the kitchen. "You're a little later than usual today."

Hope smiled. "Hullo Mamm. Joseph was late getting back from the fields."

Hope hoped that Gott would forgive her the white lie. She couldn't exactly confess to her mother that she had taken her time walking home because her employer's gratitude and smile had swept her off her feet.

"And how is Isaac? Did you have fun today?"

Hope nodded with a goofy grin. "We did. We washed the windows."

Her mother laughed as she turned to Hope. "I take it a soap sud fight ensued?"

"Jah, why else would you want to wash windows? Without a soap sud fight, it's just plain hard work."

"Exactly. You seem to enjoy taking care of him?"

"I do, Mamm. I think that his bruder has been having a hard time trying to keep Isaac entertained while he works on the farm. Luckily, I've had a lot of experience keeping kinner busy while getting some work done. You taught me how."

"I'm glad I taught you something useful." Her mother smiled. "Now be useful and set the table. I have no idea where Louisa and Rose are off to."

Hope did as she was told and set the table. As she worked, she found herself thinking of Joseph and Isaac again. What did they do in the evenings when she wasn't there? Did they play or read?

Did Joseph spend time with his little brother, or did he simply put him to bed?

After her first day taking care of Isaac, Hope had looked forward to seeing him every day. But as she set the last plate on the dinner table, she realized she was looking forward to seeing Joseph tomorrow.

PLANNING FOR THE FUTURE

"Isaac, the food was delicious. I didn't know you could cook like this?" Beth said smiling at Joseph from across the table.

"I can't," Joseph admitted with a shrug. "Hope did."

"Hope?" Beth asked confused before she nodded. "The nanny, jah?"

"Jah." Joseph confirmed. "She's taken to cooking for us most days. Although I insisted, she doesn't have to cook for us. She does more than enough as it is."

"Can I have more 'tatoes?" Isaac asked.

"Sure," Joseph added more potatoes to Isaac's plate before he returned his gaze to Beth. "I thought I'd invite you to dinner to make up for missing our buggy ride on Saturday. Mrs. Swartz was down with a cold."

Beth nodded with a heavy sigh. "I would've enjoyed the buggy ride but being invited to dinner… it's a welcome step forward in our relationship. It's been… stagnant for a while now."

Joseph didn't miss out on the jibe. Before his parents had passed away, Joseph had been ready to propose to Beth. She had hinted at a proposal with every buggy ride. But when he became

Isaac's guardian and had to take over the farm, Joseph put proposing on the back burner, knowing he needed to focus on his brother and taking over the farm.

"Hopefully, not for much longer," Joseph promised her.

Ever since Hope had begun to take care of Isaac, Joseph was finally feeling as if he had reached steady ground again. He no longer felt rushed or as if the chores were constantly falling behind. Instead, for the first time in year, he felt as if he was getting ahead.

"Are you thinking about the future again?" Beth asked hopefully.

Joseph nodded. "A little…"

Beth's eyes widened with excitement. "And what exactly have you been thinking about?"

"Beth, did you see Hope and I washed the windows?" Isaac asked, eager to be involved in the conversation.

"Jah," Beth said shortly, not even meeting Isaac's gaze. "Joseph?"

Joseph pushed away from the table and smiled at Beth. "Why don't you put on a fresh pot of kaffe, while I go and tuck Isaac in and read his bedtime story?"

"Does he have to get a story tonight?" Beth frowned with disappointment.

"Jah, he gets one every night," Joseph explained before scooping Isaac up and tossing him over his shoulder like a bag of potatoes. "Kumm, let's get you to bed."

"I must brush my teeth, first. Or the army of germs will win!" Isaac laughed as Joseph tickled him.

"Just hurry," Beth called after him.

Joseph didn't hurry at all. Putting Isaac to bed was the highlight of his day. They would read a story before Joseph would teach Isaac something from the bible. Then they would pray together, and

Joseph would tuck him in.

After his parents had passed away, Joseph had quickly learned that if Isaac didn't have that routine at night, he would sleep restlessly, and the following day would be a difficult one.

After about twenty minutes he returned to find Beth on the porch with their coffee.

"It's cold by now," Beth complained.

Joseph shrugged. "That's alright, I'm used to my kaffe getting cold with Isaac around."

He took a seat before he reached for his cup.

"You said you were thinking about our future?" Beth probed again.

"Jah, I wanted to talk to you about that. I'd like us to live here. This house… it has a lot of sentimental value for both Isaac and I," Joseph explained.

Beth frowned. "But Daed offered to build us a haus on his land?"

"I know, Beth, you've mentioned that. But I don't want to live on your daed's land. I want to continue the legacy my familye has here. The legacy that's been passed to Isaac and I."

Beth sighed heavily. "I guess I can understand that. But there will have to be some changes made."

"What changes?" Joseph asked, confused.

"The haus, Joseph. It's not at all what I'm used to. We'll need to change the kitchen completely. Ever since Daed bought Mamm the gas stove, cooking is a pleasure. The pantry needs to be extended, at the moment its nothing more than a hole in the wall, and don't get me started on the floors. The wooden floors are terribly old," Beth continued. "We should definitely consider either tiling them or having linoleum put in."

Joseph wasn't sure why she needed to change the entire kitchen, but then he wasn't a woman. His mother had never complained, he thought with a frown. "I guess we can discuss some of those changes."

"Gut. Then we'll need to add a separate bathroom, one that

only you and I use. I'm not sharing a bathroom with a five-year-old." Beth said firmly.

"What's wrong with sharing a bathroom?" Joseph asked, completely baffled.

"He's your familye, Joseph, not mine. I'd like to have at least a little privacy." Beth shrugged as if her comment wasn't meant to be hurtful.

"Perhaps we should wait to discuss the changes you'd like to make until you've lived here for a year. Maybe the haus will grow on you?" Joseph suggested hopefully.

Beth huffed. "Like money grows on trees."

Joseph smiled but didn't reply.

He couldn't help but think about Hope. Ever since she'd been working for him, it was as if his haus felt like a home again. Hope hadn't once complained about the house, the wooden floors or access to a gas stove. Joseph quickly chastened himself, realizing he couldn't compare the nanny to his sweetheart.

It was Hope's presence that had made him think about considering marriage again. He had put it on hold for such a long time, but now that he knew how much it helped to have a woman in the house, especially to help with Isaac, he realized he was ready to commit to Beth.

He so enjoyed their buggy rides and conversations and if they were married, he wouldn't have to wait for a buggy ride to talk to her. They would share their home, their lives, their hopes, and their dreams. Joseph felt excited again about his future, something he hadn't been for a very long time.

He glanced at Beth and wondered if she felt the same way. He could understand that Isaac wasn't her familye, but surely, she would care for him once they were married?

For a moment he wanted to ask her just that but decided against it. The last thing he wanted Beth to think was that he wanted to marry her for access to childcare, because that wasn't it all. He wanted to ask for her hand because he felt deep affection for her.

"Tell me about this nanny, it seems Isaac is quite taken with her?" Beth asked, interrupting the silence.

Joseph shrugged. "He is. She was the right person for the job. She's patient with him and although I don't expect it of her, she cleans and cooks for us as well. She's even taken over doing our laundry."

"She's probably eager to please you. I can't place her, have we met?" Beth asked with a frown.

Joseph frowned. "I'm not sure. Her last name is Maas."

"Widow or married?" Beth probed.

"Neither. She's barely nineteen years old. We were in the seventh grade when she started the first grade, so I doubt you've met."

"Nineteen? I thought you'd find someone like Mrs. Brahms again?" Beth asked, surprised.

"That was the plan, but the bishop suggested Hope and I can understand why. She's the eldest of five kinner and clearly enjoys taking care of them."

"I see," Beth said as if she didn't see at all. "Does she know we're courting?"

Joseph chuckled. "I didn't exactly add current courtships to our introduction."

"You should have. She sounds a little desperate. If a young girl is willing to work that hard, she must have other plans. Are they poor?"

"Beth, don't you think that's a little out of line?" Joseph quickly chastened her with a fond smile.

Joseph had known Beth long enough to know that every now and then her parents' wealth affected her judgment, but deep down he knew she was a kind person.

"I was just wondering," Beth shrugged innocently.

"It's getting late," Joseph pointed out. He had enjoyed having

Beth over for dinner, but her naivety was testing his patience tonight. He couldn't help but feel protective towards Hope and frustrated with Beth's judgement of her.

"Jah, I should get going before Daed becomes upset," Beth said with a firm nod.

"I'm sorry I can't walk you home," Joseph apologized as he stood up.

"You don't have to; I'll call for a driver." Beth shrugged as if paying someone to drive her home wasn't a luxury at all.

Joseph walked her to the phone shanty where she called for a driver. With the house in view, Joseph waited with her for ten minutes before a car arrived.

Beth turned to him with her sweet smile. "Denke for dinner, Joseph. I look forward to our plans for the future."

Joseph returned her smile. "So do I."

As the car drove away, Joseph found himself wondering if Beth would be able to accept that once they were married, luxuries such as calling for a car simply wouldn't be possible.

GREEN – THE COLOR OF ENVY

Hope had brought along paint, paper, and numerous paintbrushes this morning. As much as Isaac needed to learn the importance of doing chores, math, and learning how to read, he needed to have fun as well.

Today, that was Hope's plan.

She began the morning by cleaning the kitchen, surprised to find an extra plate in the sink. It was the first time in the month she had been working for Joseph, that he had had a guest over for dinner. Not thinking much of it, she continued with the morning chores.

Once the house was set to rights, the kitchen dealt with, and all the chores done, it was almost noon. With Isaac's help they made lunch for Joseph, before packing a picnic basket for themselves. Isaac had no idea what she was up to, but she could see that he was excited by the change in routine.

Armed with her canvas bag of painting things and a picnic basket, she led Isaac to the front yard.

"Welcome to our first ever painting picnic!" Hope announced with a clap of her hands.

"We're going to paint a picnic?" Isaac asked tilting his head, looking quite confused.

Hope smiled affectionately at him. "Nee, silly. We're going to have a picnic and paint. See that bag? I brought all my painting things with me."

"I don't know how to paint," Isaac pouted.

"Then I'll teach you. It's fun," Hope promised as she laid out their picnic blanket. She began to unpack the basket containing their lunch, some fruit, as well as cool drinks. She had also packed two mason jars with water for them to use to rinse their brushes. With everything set up, she finally reached for the canvas bag.

Because Hope and her siblings enjoyed painting so much, her father had long ago cut two pieces of wood into boards, they could use as backing when they painted on paper. Hope clipped a page to each board and handed one to Isaac. "Here you go."

Isaac accepted the board with a frown. "But it's white?"

Hope laughed. "That's why we're going to paint it, any color you want."

Once all the paint and brushes had been laid out, Hope demonstrated how to use the paint. She dipped a paint brush in a mason jar and dabbed the paint before drawing a circle on the page. "See, it's easy."

Isaac eagerly followed her example. Before long he was enjoying the painting just as Hope had enjoyed it when she was a young girl.

They painted flowers, trees, and Hope even helped Isaac to paint his name. With the sun on her back and the laughter of a little boy beside her, Hope couldn't remember the last time she had so much fun.

"Let's give those pages a chance to dry while we have some lunch," Hope suggested as she handed Isaac a sandwich.

Isaac eagerly accepted the sandwich. Clearly, he had forgotten all about lunch until she had offered him food. "When we're done eating, can we paint the house?"

Hope nodded as she took a bite of her sandwich. When she was done chewing, she smiled at Isaac. "We can paint it together, what do you say?"

"Jah!" Isaac cried out with excitement. "And then I can give it to Joseph. Maybe he'll put it on the fridge, we have magnets."

"That's a wunderbaar idea," Hope agreed.

"What's a wunderbaar idea?"

Hope turned at the sound of Joseph's voice. She had made it a point not to interact with him unless necessary since that evening when he had smiled at her in the kitchen. Because now every time he did, she felt that same twist in her belly before her heart began to race.

It wasn't appropriate, especially since he had a sweetheart.

"We're going to paint the house," Hope explained, quickly breaking eye contact.

"That sounds like fun. I still wanted to thank you for dinner last night, Hope. It was very gut," Joseph complimented her with a bright smile.

Why was it that when he did that, her heart stopped before it began to speed up as if it was in a derby? "It's a pleasure to cook in such a lovely kitchen."

Joseph frowned oddly before he nodded. "If you say so?"

"Is something wrong?" Hope asked at his strange expression.

"Nee, nee, it's... nothing. Enjoy your picnic," Joseph said before he headed inside to get his lunch.

"Right, let's finish lunch and start painting the house," Hope said to distract herself from Joseph's brief presence and her reaction to it.

* * *

JOSEPH STEPPED into the kitchen and looked around. In his opinion the kitchen had always been more than sufficient. Although the ordnung permitted gas-operated appliances, Joseph still felt it was a little modern for his taste. It wasn't that he judged anyone who had a gas stove, he just didn't feel it was necessary to make such an excessive purchase.

His gaze drifted to the wood floors and a smile curved his mouth. Although the floors were worn, they were in good condition. As his eyes travelled over the floorboards, numerous memories washed over him. The black stain by the wood stove was from when his father had stoked the coals when Joseph had been young, and a coal had dropped onto the floor.

Beneath the table he would always remember the dusting of flour that spilled there when his mother baked cookies. Then there was the pantry. It had been his favorite hiding space as a child.

The ice box against the far wall of the pantry had been built by his father. Although they now had a fridge that worked on propane, Joseph still used the ice box for vegetables and fruit.

He recalled Beth's comments from last night and Hope's compliment a few moments ago.

Each woman had a completely different opinion of his kitchen, and it bothered Joseph that his opinion aligned more with the nanny's than with his sweetheart's.

Pushing thoughts of Beth and Hope aside, he uncovered the plate where his sandwiches lay waiting for him. As he took the first bite, he could hear Hope and Isaac's conversation float in through the kitchen window.

"Hope, what is your favorite color?" Isaac asked.

"All of them," Hope said simply.

Isaac moved towards the window, taking his plate with him. He wasn't exactly spying on them, he just happened to be looking in the direction where they were sitting.

Isaac giggled, shaking his head. "All of them? You can't choose all of them, if you had to choose just one, which one would it be?"

Hope thought long and hard, pretending to struggle with a choice. "Today, if I had to choose today? Then it would be green."

"Green?" Isaac frowned. "Because it's the color of grass?"

"Nee," Hope shook her head. "Because that's the color on your nose."

Joseph smiled as he watched them. Hope really had a way with his brother. She didn't see him as bothersome or interruptive, she truly enjoyed his company. He watched as she wiped the green paint Isaac had managed to get on his nose off.

"What is your favorite color?" Hope asked when she was done.

Isaac smiled brightly. "That's easy, yellow. It was Mamm's favorite color too. The color of buttercups."

Joseph's breath caught. Ever since their parents had passed, Isaac hardly ever spoke about them. Joseph had begun to wonder if he was forgetting them.

"Your mamm had gut taste. Yellow is my favorite color at least once a week." Hope didn't coddle him because he had mentioned his mother, instead she continued the conversation. "Do you know why I like all the colors?"

"Why?" Isaac asked as he reached for his paint brush, eager to start painting again.

"Because Gott made all of them. I like green because it's the color of trees, I like red because it's the color of roses. I like pink because it's the color of piglets, and I like blue because it's the color of the sky."

"And black because it's the color of the sky after dark?" Isaac asked.

Hope nodded. "And orange because it's the color of oranges."

Isaac giggled as they continued their little game. "And brown because it's the color of dirt."

Joseph smiled as he watched them. For a moment he felt like

an outsider looking in. He would've liked nothing more than to join them on their picnic, but there was Beth to consider. It had been clear in her comments the night before that she didn't approve of such a young girl spending time at Joseph's house.

If only Beth could see how happy Hope's presence made Isaac, Joseph thought before he turned away from the window to finish his lunch.

TRUST IN THE LORD

Saturday morning Hope was surprised to feel disappointed that she wouldn't be heading to the Yoder house that day. She had come to enjoy her time with Isaac so much, that it felt strange knowing that she wouldn't be seeing him today.

A strange type of melancholy hung over her when she finally climbed out of bed. Saturdays used to be her favorite day of the week, but instead of looking forward to spending a whole day with her family, she found herself longing to spend the day with another family instead.

Before she even got dressed, Hope kneeled before her bed and clasped her hands in prayer. She had tried to ignore the way that she felt when Joseph was around, but it hadn't worked. Now it was time for prayer.

Hopefully if she begged Gott to remove the feelings that had grown inside her heart without intent, he would bless her and relieve her of them.

. . .

"GOTT, I kneel before you this morning grateful to have been blessed with another day. Denke for my familye, for our health, and for all the blessings you bestow on us each day. Gott, only you know what is in my heart, only you know how unfit these feelings are.

I have been hired to care for Isaac, Gott, and I do care for him, deeply, but I find myself caring for his bruder as well. Gott, it is a sin to covet what belongs to another... Please forgive me of this sin. Joseph and Beth are on the verge of becoming engaged and these feelings I have for him are unsuitable to say the least.

I beg of you to wash my heart clean of the attraction and affection I feel for him, Gott. I beg of you, to steel my heart against developing such feelings for him in future and to focus my time and my attention on Isaac and only Isaac. I ask this not because I am deserving of your mercy and blessings, Gott, because I am a follower of your teachings. Amen."

HOPE DRESSED for the day and made a list of all the chores that she could get done today. Although her mother and siblings kept abreast of most of the chores since Hope began working outside of the home, she still felt it her duty to contribute.

After breakfast she began by sweeping the porch before she headed inside to give the woodstove a good clean.

Before she could start, her mother joined her in the kitchen. "There you are, guten mayrie my dochder."

"Guten mayrie Mamm, how are you this morning?" Hope asked as she poured her mother a cup of coffee.

"Gut, I completely overslept and your daed and I have a meeting with the other deacons in just an hour."

Hope smiled. "You deserve to sleep in every now and then."

"So do you," her mother said with a firm look. "You've been working so hard these last few weeks; you deserve to rest a little. I don't think you realize how much your daed and I appreciate the wages you contribute towards the household."

"I'm glad it offers relief." Hope smiled at her mother. It felt good to know that she was finally making a difference in her parents' lives and not just being a burden anymore.

"Your bruder has plans to help a friend today, so I was hoping you could watch the young ones? I thought maybe you might spoil them and take them into town for lunch and perhaps an ice cream?"

"Is that necessary? It's an extravagant expense, Mamm," Hope cautioned her mother.

"We can afford it. Besides, both you and they deserve it. They've missed you terribly these last few weeks."

Hope hesitated but she knew her mother was right. "Alright, I'll take Daniel and Rose into town for lunch and an ice cream. Maybe we'll spend the afternoon painting when we get back."

"They'll enjoy that. You're a gut schweschder, Hope. Always remember that," Her mother insisted.

Hope smiled at her mother weakly. "Denke Mamm, but does that mean I always make the right choices?" Hope asked. She didn't want to tell her mother about her feelings for Joseph, but perhaps her mother could give her advice.

"Nee, being a gut person, a faithful person, doesn't mean you make all the right choices. It just means that when you make the wrong ones, you learn from them. Remember Proverbs 3:5 - *Trust in the Lord with all your heart and do not lean on your understanding.* I believe that if we do that, Gott will lead us towards the right decisions."

Hope nodded in agreement. Her mother was right. She should stop worrying about the way she felt about Joseph and instead trust in the Lord. He understood her heart and he could relieve her of any affection she had developed for Joseph.

"Denke Mamm, that's the best advice you've ever given me."

"Really? I thought the best advice I ever gave you was how to get tomato stains out of white shirts?"

Hope and her mother's laughter filled the kitchen.

AWKWARD SILENCES

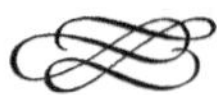

"**I**s he coming with?" Beth asked, surprised to see Isaac sitting in the buggy beside Joseph.

Joseph smiled brightly at his sweetheart. "I thought instead of our usual buggy ride, I could treat my two favorite people to ice cream?"

Beth's smile remained in place as Joseph helped her into the buggy.

This morning he had considered asking Mrs. Schwartz to look after Isaac while he went on his buggy ride with Beth that afternoon, but instead he had decided against it. It wasn't fair to Isaac to stay home when Joseph planned on going for ice cream.

The weather had really warmed up over the last couple of weeks and with the warmer weather returned Joseph's love for ice cream.

"That's a generous idea," Beth said, looking at Joseph over Isaac's head.

"I want to get the pepper chocolate. That's my favorite," Isaac informed her with a smile.

Joseph laughed. "It's peppermint chocolate."

"Jah, peppermint chocolate. What flavor do you like?" Isaac asked her.

Joseph kept his eyes on the road, wondering if it was disappointment he heard in Beth's voice when he said he was taking her and Isaac for ice cream. He knew she liked ice cream so the only reason for her disappointment could be Isaac.

He quickly shoved the thought aside. Beth had never had a problem with Isaac, why would she have one now? She understood that Joseph was Isaac's guardian and that when they married, Isaac would stay with them.

"Actually, I don't really care for ice cream that much," Beth replied stiffly.

Joseph turned to Beth with a curious look. "You've always liked ice cream, haven't you?"

"I've outgrown it," Beth shrugged, quickly looking away.

Joseph didn't allow her comment to bother him too much, perhaps she was just having a bad day.

A short while later he stopped the buggy in front of the diner. There were three diners in town, but this one had the best ice cream in Joseph's opinion. Once they were seated a waitress appeared at their table, chewing gum as she spoke. "What'll it be?"

"Pepper chocolate ice cream please." Isaac answered first.

Joseph laughed and turned to the waitress. "He means, peppermint chocolate. I'll have the butter pecan, please. What would you like, Beth?"

Beth held her silence for a long moment, almost long enough for it to become uncomfortable before she spoke. "I'll have chocolate ice cream."

"I thought you didn't like ice cream?" Isaac asked with a frown.

"Didn't you outgrow it?" Joseph teased.

"Perhaps now that we're here, I've simply changed my mind," Beth said curtly with a huff of impatience.

"That happens," Joseph agreed. "How was your week?"

Beth glanced at Isaac before she answered Joseph. "Tiring. I was looking forward to a quiet buggy ride."

Joseph understood the meaning of her words. She didn't expect to spend the afternoon with his little brother. He felt a little guilty for not checking with her first, perhaps it had been insensitive of him to make plans without consulting her. He was about to apologize when Isaac spoke.

"Here it comes!"

Joseph laughed at his little brother's excitement. Although Isaac was only five years old, it felt as if Joseph couldn't remember a time when his little brother hadn't been part of his life.

Joseph had been an only child for twenty years before his parents announced the joyous news of the arrival of a baby. Later Joseph had learned that his parents had tried all those years but had never been blessed, until Isaac had come along.

Isaac had been the late comer his parents had prayed for, and the sibling that Joseph had always wanted. Of course, he had never thought that his role as big brother would become the role of a guardian, but he still didn't mind.

Once the waitress had delivered their orders, Joseph made numerous attempts at conversation with Beth. But her responses remained single syllables or simply nods. What Joseph had hoped would be a great opportunity for Beth and Isaac to get to know each other, turned out to be an awkward affair.

He was about to suggest it was time for them to leave when Isaac jumped out of the booth and ran across the diner.

"Isaac!" Joseph called out after his brother. Before Joseph could get out of the booth, he saw the reason for his brother's excitement.

Hope.

"It's Hope. Come, I'd like to introduce you," Joseph said as he shifted out of the booth.

"Hope? Oh, the nanny." Beth's voice lilted up with the last part.

As they approached Hope's booth, Joseph listened as she asked Isaac about his day and what type of ice cream he had. Only when he reached them did he notice two other children with her.

"Hullo Hope," Joseph greeted her with a smile. "This is Beth, my...sweetheart."

"Hullo. It's such a pleasure to meet you, Beth," Hope said, slipping out of the booth for the introductions. "This is my brother, Daniel, and my sister, Rose."

"We're going to go and paint!" Rose announced excitedly.

Hope turned to her sister with a playful smile. "Not if you interrupt the grownups."

"And I'm Isaac!" Isaac introduced himself without invitation.

"We were just about to leave, but it was nice to meet you, Beth. Isaac, I'll see you Monday morning." Hope reached for her purse as her siblings began to slide out of the booth.

"Are we going to paint now?" Rose asked again.

"Jah, when we get home," Hope laughed.

"I want to paint too, can I come?" Isaac asked hopefully.

"If your bruder agrees, we'd love to have you," Hope answered without hesitation.

Joseph's heart was warmed by her eagerness to spend time with his brother. "I'm sure that will be fine. I'll come by to fetch him later?"

"Perfect," Hope nodded.

"Denke," Beth said, surprising Joseph as she turned to Hope. "It's hard to have a conversation with him around."

Hope's eyes narrowed but she kept her smile in place. "I'm sure it is. Bye now."

Joseph watched his brother leave with Hope and her siblings and for a moment wished he could go with them. Hope had an energy about her that pulled you closer. A type of energy that was almost magnetic as it was contagious.

"Thank heavens, finally I get to spend some time alone with you," Beth said with a sigh of relief.

Joseph turned to her with a curious look. "You do realize that when we're married, Isaac is always going to be around."

Beth's eyes widened for a moment before she eased the look away with a smile. "All the more reason for me to want to spend time alone with you now."

Joseph didn't question her further, instead he led her back to their booth and slid in. He had barely taken a seat before Beth became the chatterbox he was used to. As he listened to her with one ear, he wondered if children in general made her uncomfortable, or was it just Isaac?

THE HONESTY OF YOUNG MINDS

After dropping Beth off at home, Joseph headed to the Maas homestead. Hope had explained to him where she lived on a previous occasion, but he had never been there before. He took his time, not hurrying the horse at all, since he found his mind spilling over with numerous questions and decisions about the future.

If hiring Hope had made Joseph realize one thing, it was that Isaac needed a mother figure in his life. His brother simply blossomed with Hope's care and attention, making it clear that he missed the gentle touch and affection that only a woman could give.

It was because of that reason that he had decided to take Beth and Isaac out together today. In his mind he had thought they would get along and that Beth would simply adore Isaac. Instead, she had seemed blatantly irritated with Isaac's presence.

But not even her behavior was enough for Joseph to consider that she might not like his brother. Instead, he firmly believed that he had been wrong to arrange it without asking her first. Next time he would talk to her ahead of time and explain his reasoning.

If they planned on spending the rest of their lives together, it would be good for Isaac and Beth to get to know each other.

For the last year, Joseph had put off getting engaged and now that he had finally found his feet after the tragedy that cost him his parents, he was ready to start moving ahead with his future. That future would include Beth and hopefully a family of their own.

Joseph couldn't help but feel excited about the future. Losing his parents had been a terrible loss, but he knew that his parents wouldn't want him to mourn forever, they would've encouraged him to embrace his life and provide a loving home for his brother.

And that was just what Joseph was going to do. He would talk with Beth and arrange a few visits that would include Isaac, that way they wouldn't be strangers to each other when the wedding took place. It was spring in Lancaster County now, but Joseph hoped that before autumn arrived with her paintbrushes and painted all the trees, he would be a married man.

He pulled into the Maas homestead and could hear the laughter of children even before he climbed out of the buggy. Following the laughter, he rounded the barn and couldn't help but smile at the sight that met him.

A trestle table had been set up against the side of the barn and above it hung numerous paintings drying in the sun. There were pictures of flowers, fruits, and even what looked to be a mangled horse. But that wasn't what made him smile.

It was the sight of Isaac playing catch with Hope's siblings while she put the painting things away. He couldn't remember the last time Isaac had played with other children. Since he didn't go to a daycare, Isaac's interaction with other children tended to be very limited.

"Ach!" Hope cried out suddenly. "You gave me a terrible fright, Joseph. You should've said you were here."

Joseph shrugged with a foolish smile. "Sorry, I was distracted by the sight of Isaac playing with kinner his own age. Since his brother is twenty years older than him, I'm sure he misses the company of other kinner."

"They have been talking, painting, and playing ever since we arrived home. How was your... visit with Beth?" Hope asked as she rinsed all the paint brushes.

"Very nice, denke. Denke for allowing Isaac to come with you. I really appreciate the way you always make him feel welcome."

"That's because he is. He's going to be exhausted tonight. They've been running for about the last thirty minutes." Hope laughed. "Where they get the energy – I have no idea."

"I was just thinking the same thing," Joseph admitted. "Isaac, kumm."

Isaac smiled at the sight of Joseph and ran straight towards him. "Did you see my paintings, Joseph?"

"I did, they're very gut," Joseph complimented his brother as he pointed to the mangled horse. "Come on, it's time for us to head home. Say gutbye."

Once everyone had bid farewell, Joseph and Isaac pulled out of the yard.

Joseph considered his words carefully before he finally spoke. "Did you enjoy playing with Hope's siblings?"

"Jah, I wish I could have siblings," Isaac pouted and crossed his arms.

"When I marry, I plan on having a lot of kinner. They'll be your siblings, actually more like nieces and nephews, but still, you can play with them," Joseph promised.

"If you get married will a woman share your room, like Mamm and Daed did?"

"Jah, and she'll live with us. She'll be almost like a mother to you, only she'll never take Mamm's place," Joseph explained.

Isaac thought for a time before he finally spoke again. "Do you get to choose who you want to marry?"

"Jah, of course, it's my decision. Long time ago it was that a matchmaker chose for you, but these days we're free to marry whom we choose."

"And who have you chosen?" Isaac asked with hopeful eyes.

"Actually, I haven't asked for her hand yet, but I hope to ask for it soon. I've chosen Beth. She's kind and caring and will be a great mamm one day."

Isaac's frown deepened. "Beth? But she's not nice. She doesn't even like me and she lied about ice cream. It's bad to tell lies."

"Wait a minute, you only met her today. Beth is very nice, and she does like you. And she didn't lie about ice cream, she simply changed her mind," Joseph explained gently. "You don't know her like I do, once you do, you'll like her as well."

"But you can choose?" Isaac asked again.

"Jah. That's what I said."

"Then choose Hope. She's nice and friendly and likes me. She makes nice food, and she paints with me and she likes ice cream. She can come and live with us instead of going home every night. Then she can tuck me into bed and read me bedtime stories..." Isaac explained at a mile a minute.

Joseph's eyes widened with surprise. "Slow down, bruder. Like I said, the choice is mine. Although Hope is everything you just said, she isn't my sweetheart."

Isaac shrugged as if that was a minor detail. "Then choose her as your sweetheart."

Joseph let out a heavy sigh. The last thing he wanted to do was to debate with a five-year-old over his choice of wife. He had hoped to gauge Isaac's feelings with regards to Joseph getting married, he didn't want a list of reasons why he shouldn't marry Beth and why he should marry Hope instead.

He didn't scold his brother for his opinion, but he didn't allow him to expand on it further. When they arrived home, Joseph unhitched the horse and put away the buggy while Isaac headed inside to run himself a bath.

As he filled the horse's water bucket, he thought about what Isaac had said.

Would Hope make a gut wife?

KINNER ARE A BLESSING
FROM GOTT

Sunday service the following week was centered about children.

Hope listened avidly as the bishop spoke about the importance of patience, affection, and guidance to be provided by parents. It was a lovely sermon that made Hope smile and dream of the day she would be blessed to have a family of her own.

Children are a gift from the LORD, they are a reward from him. Psalm 127:3

That had been the verse for the day. It was such an apt description of how honored one should be to receive such a blessing. As the sermon continued, Hope glanced at Joseph who was sitting with the other men, with Isaac by his side.

Hope didn't doubt for one minute that although Isaac was his brother, that was how Joseph felt. He felt honored to be Isaac's guardian, although the responsibility could be overwhelming at times. Just like Hope felt blessed to be Isaac's nanny.

A smile curved her mouth, just thinking about the adorable little boy. Weekends became harder and harder when she was away from him because she had come to love Isaac. For someone who celebrated children and basked in their company, it hadn't come as a surprise.

But what had come as a surprise was that Hope felt affection for Joseph as well. Regardless of her prayers for Gott to diminish the unwanted feelings, they seemed to have taken hold of her heart. Hope did her best to keep her distance from Joseph, to avoid her feelings deepening even more.

A few rows ahead of her she spotted Beth and let out a quiet sigh. She couldn't help but wonder if Beth even realized how lucky she was to be Joseph's sweetheart. When Joseph and Beth married, she would become a mother figure to Isaac.

Jealousy washed over Hope as the service came to an end. She knew it was wrong, but it was only because she cared too much. Instead of approaching her job as a nanny with cool resolve and accepting it was only a job, she had become too involved. She had allowed herself to love Isaac and now she couldn't help but wish she would be the one to raise him.

But that was just a dream. A dream she needed to forget, she reminded herself as the service came to an end.

Once the final prayer and blessing was given, the service was over. Everyone moved out of the barn towards the refreshment tables where cookies, juice, and homemade lemonade could be found. It wasn't compulsory to stay for refreshments, but it was the community's way of reconnecting every second Sunday.

Everywhere, groups formed with people of the same interests. The sewing bee ladies gathered by the large tree, the deacons stood and spoke to the bishop, while children began to run and play eager to rid themselves of the pent-up energy after a long service.

Hope helped herself to a refreshment before she stood to one side to keep an eye on Rose. Her mother didn't have to ask her, Hope had just offered. This morning Hope didn't feel like small talk with the other women her age, she was too lost in her own thoughts and struggles.

Isaac ran towards her with a beaming grin. "Hope!"

Hope braced herself just in time before Isaac crushed into her and wrapped his arms around her legs. "Are you going to play?" he asked, looking up at her.

Hope shook her head. "Not today, but tomorrow we can play a game you've never played before," she promised.

A few feet away from her, Hope noticed Joseph and Beth talking. Beth was truly a beautiful woman, Hope admitted to herself. Her auburn hair just peeked out of the front of her prayer kapp, and Hope couldn't help but wonder how magnificent her hair must be when she let it loose to comb it out at night. Joseph laughed at something Beth said, and Hope felt a twinge of jealousy.

She quickly walked towards the children, hating the envy that had overcome her. For the first time in her life, she was eager to leave Sunday service.

She didn't want to be there, seeing Joseph fawn over Beth. She had only seen them together that one time at the coffee shop before. That day she had only liked Joseph. The deep feelings she felt for him now were no longer just a passing interest.

Hope scanned the crowd for her parents and sighed when she noticed they were still in deep discussion with other congregants. It might be a while before she could escape. She was about to sit down and watch the children when someone cried out, "fire!"

As one, the men moved towards each other to assess the smoke, wind direction, and how many men they would need to stop the fire from expanding and ravaging more farmlands.

It wasn't unusual this time of year to have fires in their area. With little rainfall over the winter, and summer rainfall yet to come, it took very little for a fire to spark, especially with their community living so close to the highway.

Men ran towards buggies, while the women began to arrange who would give whom a lift home.

The children had all dispersed to their mothers, realizing

Sunday service was over. Hope noticed Joseph walking towards Beth with Isaac by his side. They were only standing a few feet away from her.

Hope couldn't overhear the conversation, but when Joseph frowned and shook his head, she knew something wasn't right.

The next moment Joseph walked towards her with Isaac by his side. "I'm sorry to ask you, but I have no one else. Could you watch Isaac, while I go and help with the fire?"

"Of course," Hope agreed without hesitation.

"Denke, I'll come by for him after," Joseph promised before saying goodbye to Isaac.

"Don't worry, just be careful." Hope couldn't help that her voice held an edge of concern.

Joseph nodded before he jogged towards the other men.

Hope glanced down at Isaac who had slipped his hand into hers. "You're ready to come and visit at my haus?"

Isaac nodded. "I'm glad Beth had more important things to do, I didn't want to stay with her anyway."

Isaac's words shocked Hope to the core. He wouldn't have come up with that excuse on his own, which meant that Beth must have said that to Joseph in front of Isaac. She glanced at Beth and found herself questioning the woman's character.

They had just listened to a three-hour sermon on children being a blessing, a privilege, and yet she had walked out of service and told Joseph she had better things to do than watch his brother?

A heavy sigh escaped Hope. She didn't want to judge Beth, but she couldn't help but wonder what life would be like for Isaac if Beth and Joseph married. Would she always be indifferent towards Isaac, or was it just today?

"Don't worry, you are the most important thing on my list today," she promised Isaac before she moved towards her mother and her siblings.

"Hullo Isaac," her mother greeted Isaac with a warm, welcome smile. Hope had never been more grateful for her mother's kind demeanor than in that moment. Isaac needed to feel like he belonged and that he was welcome, not that he was an errand or an inconvenience.

"Hullo," Isaac smiled shyly.

"Isaac is going to come and visit with us while Joseph goes to help with the fire," Hope explained.

"That's a lovely idea," her mother agreed. "Kumm, let's get home so I can start on Sunday supper, I'm sure you kinner want to go and play?"

Hope's younger siblings and Isaac all cried out together. "Jah!"

AMISH HOSPITALITY

It had taken the effort of thirty men and four hours to completely extinguish the fire. How it began was still a mystery, but then most of the fires that started near the highway were from cigarette butts being tossed out the window by careless travelers.

Joseph loved the traditions of his community and their way of turning their backs on modern technology, but today when he had been surrounded by flames and exhausted men, he had wished for a moment that they had a truck with a fire-fighting pump on the back.

But instead, they had extinguished the fire like they had for a hundred years: by beating the flames with homemade fire-eaters.

When Joseph climbed into his buggy, he was surprised to see how late it had become. During the fire nothing had mattered except for saving lives and crops. Only now he realized it was almost four o'clock in the afternoon. He knew that Isaac would be happy and safe with Hope, so he decided a few more minutes wouldn't make a world of difference.

He was covered in soot and stank like a chimney. He would

pass his homestead on the way to the Maas homestead, so he decided to stop and wash up before he went to collect Isaac. Barely thirty minutes later, he was back in his buggy and headed to the Maas homestead.

As he held the reins with his eyes on the dirt road, he remembered Beth's horrified expression and unflappable answer when he had asked her to take care of Isaac. Her answer had been so callous that Joseph couldn't help but be offended. He only hoped that Isaac was too young to realize and hadn't taken offense himself.

Was it wrong of him to feel anger towards Beth because of it? She had reminded him numerous times that Isaac wasn't her blood, or her problem, but Joseph couldn't help but start to doubt if she would ever concern herself with Isaac.

He was only five years old and had a long way ahead of him before he would make a life of his own. Surely, Beth understood that Isaac would be part of their family.

A sigh escaped him as the Maas house came into view. He didn't have the energy to think about Beth or his future now. All he wanted was to see Isaac and thank Hope for her willingness to take care of him.

If it hadn't been for Hope…

A frown creased Joseph's brow as he realized that he could depend more on Hope than he could on the woman he hoped to marry. The thought bothered him more than he would admit.

He had barely brought the buggy to a standstill in front of the barn when Isaac and Hope's siblings came running around the house, headed straight for him.

"Did you win the fire?" Isaac asked first with wide eyes.

"Is it dead?" Daniel stepped closer, eager to learn about the fire.

Last, but not least, Rose's sweet little voice filled the air. "Did you get burned?

"Jah, jah, and nee, I didn't get burned, but denke for asking." Joseph smiled at the little girl. She took after Hope in more ways than one. For a moment Joseph wondered if Hope's daughter would look like Rose one day.

"You're back," Hope said, coming around the corner. "You must be exhausted."

"Jah, it was a tough fire, but we beat it. Did Isaac behave himself?" Joseph asked with teasing grin for his brother.

"Of course, he did, he is always on his best behavior," Hope extrapolated with dramatic effect.

"Gut to hear. We'll be on our way, once again, denke for taking him. I really appreciate it," Joseph said, meeting Hope's gaze.

She smiled at him with kindness that confirmed her words. "It was only a pleasure. He's welcome here any time."

"My cookie!" Isaac said suddenly. "You have to see my cookie!"

Hope laughed. "He's right, you must see his cookie. Mamm allowed them to use her special food paint to paint cookies."

"Then I guess I need to come and see the cookie," Joseph chuckled as he followed Hope and the children towards the house.

After greeting Hope's parents, Joseph couldn't help but appreciate how homey the Maas home felt. It wasn't large and some of the furniture had seen better days, but it was a home that was filled with love.

Isaac showed him a star-shaped cookie he had painted in all the colors of the rainbow, eagerly explaining the reasoning behind each color.

"Once again, denke. I hope you have a blessed day further," Joseph greeted the Maas family.

"You can't leave now," Mrs. Maas said, moving towards him. "It's almost time for dinner and I already cooked for both you and Isaac. We know how long these fires can take and when you're done, you're exhausted. You'll stay for supper."

"I really don't mean to impose," Joseph began to decline.

"It's an imposition if you invite yourself, but I just invited you. Besides, I'm sure the last thing you feel like doing now is to go home and cook dinner?"

Joseph shrugged; he couldn't argue with that.

Although Joseph had never met Hope's family before, within minutes he felt as if they were old friends. Everyone made him feel welcome and clearly doted over Isaac. It warmed Joseph's heart to see how at home Isaac was amongst the Maas family. He played with Daniel and Rose and looked up at Peter as a role model.

When they sat down for dinner, Joseph hoped that Isaac wouldn't fuss over all the vegetables on his plate. He didn't say a single word. Instead, he ate his vegetables, just like Daniel and Rose.

The food was delicious, and the best part about the meal was seeing Hope in her natural environment. Surrounded by her family she seemed different.

She was more relaxed and happier. When she was at his home, she seemed almost wary, but here her laughter came easily, just as teasing her siblings came without second thought.

Joseph was more than a little charmed by this side of Hope. He could understand his brother's infatuation with his nanny a little better. It was easy to see that as the eldest sibling she held as much authority over the younger children as her parents and yet they adored her. There was a lot of love surrounding this table, Joseph realized as he finished his plate of food.

His thoughts drifted back to Beth and the only time he had been invited for dinner at her parents' house. It had been before his parents had passed away.

Dinner there had been a little stiff and much quieter than dinner at the Maas table. Mrs. and Mrs. Stoltzfus barely said a word all through dinner. Joseph had just accepted it was because he was a stranger at their table.

But the way he and Isaac were being received at the Maas table was completely opposite from what he had experienced at the Stoltzfus house.

He still couldn't believe that Beth had outright refused to look after Isaac this afternoon. Did she dislike Isaac or children in general? Joseph pushed the thought aside, he wouldn't judge her because of her behavior. Once again, he had caught her off guard, just like when she had acted strange when he had taken her for ice cream with Isaac.

Perhaps if he planned something ahead, gave her fair warning, she would be warmer towards Isaac.

After dinner, Mr. Maas invited Joseph to enjoy coffee with him on the porch while the women handled the cleaning of the kitchen. For some reason Joseph had expected there would be a few firm words coming from the kitchen, but instead Hope turned it into a game.

By the time the kitchen was done, and Joseph's coffee was finished, he knew it was time for them to leave. Isaac still needed to take a bath and he was already yawning after an afternoon filled with fun and playtime.

After he said goodbye to everyone, Hope followed him and Isaac to the buggy. Joseph lifted Isaac into the buggy and handed him his jacket. Isaac nearly drowned in the large jacket, but it didn't bother him. He curled up onto the buggy seat and closed his eyes.

"I doubt you're going to be able to give him a bath tonight, let me deal with it tomorrow morning. He's exhausted," Hope said quietly as she smiled at his brother.

"Jah, you're probably right. He had so much fun." Joseph searched Hope's gaze and frowned. "You're different when you're home."

Hope frowned. "How do you mean? I'm just me." Her shoulders lifted before they dropped again.

Joseph shook his head. "Nee, you are different. You laugh easier and you seem happier. When you're at my haus… it's almost as if you're wary… afraid of something, if I can put it like that for lack of a better explanation."

Hope's eyes widened for a moment before she shook her head. "You're imagining things. Besides, this is my haus, my familye, it's only natural for me to be comfortable around them."

"So, you're not comfortable around me?" Joseph prodded. He wasn't sure why, but he wanted Hope to be comfortable around him and not just around his brother.

Hope went quiet for a moment before she met his gaze. "You are my employer, Joseph. I'm just trying to keep a proper distance…" She trailed off as if she wanted to say something else.

Joseph took a step forward. "I'd like to think of us more as friends."

"You want us to be friends?" Hope asked with a frown.

"Jah," Joseph answered without hesitation.

Hope didn't say a word, instead she searched his gaze as if she was searching for a reason to be his friend. Joseph couldn't give her one. He wasn't sure why he wanted to be her friend either. He had a sweetheart, and he had friends.

But for some reason he was drawn by Hope. He found himself searching her hazel gaze for a reason, but he didn't need one. She was the reason, everything about her.

Attraction caught him off guard, just as the connection he felt with Hope completely took his breath away. This wasn't something he had expected and now that he realized it, he felt baffled by it.

"Joseph…." Isaac's sleepy voice came from the buggy.

Hope quickly took a step back and summoned the smile it seemed she reserved for him: it was friendly but not completely real. "Drive safe, Joseph."

Joseph nodded as he saw her fall back into the cool and wary Hope she was when she was at his home. "Sleep well, Hope. Once again, denke for today."

Hope nodded before she turned and walked back towards the house. Joseph climbed into the buggy, but he glanced at the Maas house with longing. Not just for Hope, but for the family she had.

One day, he hoped he could give that to Isaac.

EYES ARE WINDOWS TO THE SOUL

As the weeks passed and the weather grew warmer, the corn reached for the sky. When Hope had begun working for Joseph, he had just seeded and now the fields were filled with green stalks holding the promise of a good harvest.

Just like she had come to love Isaac and have feelings for Joseph, Hope had come to care about the farm. She had witnessed how much work and effort Joseph had put into his fields this year. Just as Joseph prayed for a good harvest, Hope prayed for the same every night.

But just as she prayed for Joseph's harvest and for him and Isaac's wellbeing, she prayed that Gott would harden her heart against the feelings that seemed to grow with every passing day. Hope was disappointed in herself because of the feelings she had for Joseph. His engagement to Beth was imminent and when it happened Hope knew her heart would break.

If it wasn't bad enough that she had feelings for Joseph and had come to care for Isaac as if he were her own, there was the evening beside the barn at her house. That night when she had walked Joseph and Isaac to buggy, something had changed between her and Joseph.

He had looked at her in a way that made her feel as if she was the only woman in the world. For a moment she had imagined what it would be like to have Joseph's affections, to be the one he would propose to.

She couldn't be sure, but she was almost certain that he had felt something that night as well.

Hope tried not to think back to that evening too much, because every time she did, she felt guilty. Instead, she focused on her job and spent more time cleaning than necessary, fearing that an idle moment would expose her to a second alone with Joseph, something she had avoided ever since that night.

Hope didn't want to know if Joseph had feelings for her, it would only make the entire situation even harder than it already was. She had debated resigning, but simply couldn't get it in her heart to say goodbye to Isaac. Just like Isaac needed her, she had come to need him. She celebrated his achievements and milestones and wanted to remain part of his life.

Whatever had transpired between her and Joseph that night could only lead to one thing, Joseph terminating her services.

"There, I did it, see?" Isaac said, holding up his piece of paper.

Hope smiled when he interrupted her thoughts. She was grateful for the distraction. She took the page from Isaac and inspected it, pretending to be very thorough. This afternoon, instead of playing or painting, Hope had decided to give him another writing lesson.

As with everything Isaac attempted, he did it with curiosity and excitement. Today she was teaching him how to write his name. The letters were a little squiggly and not at all neat, but she could read the word *Isaac*.

Hope's mouth curved into a proud smile. "You did it! You wrote your name for the very first time. Well done, Isaac, I'm so proud of you."

Isaac's mouth split his face in two as he smiled at his achievement. "Can I learn how to write your name now?"

Hope laughed. "If you really want? But perhaps you want to practice writing your name instead?"

"Nee, I want to write your name," Isaac said firmly.

Patiently Hope taught him how to draw the letters of her name. Isaac copied the letters a few times, before he began to write her name. When he was done, he handed her the page. "That's for you."

Hope's eyes welled with tears at the beautiful moment. One day she hoped to tell Isaac how touched she was that the second word he ever wrote had been her name. "Denke Isaac, it's perfect."

Isaac's chest puffed out with pride. "I'm going to go show Joseph."

Before Hope could stop him, Isaac took the page with his name on it and rushed down the porch towards the field where Joseph was working.

After gathering their writing things and the extra paper that Hope kept for his lessons, Hope headed inside to put them away in the sideboard. Just as she was about to step out onto the porch again, Joseph came through the door.

Before Hope could lose her balance from the unexpected impact, Joseph grabbed her arms and steadied her. "I'm sorry, I didn't see you there. Are you alright?" Joseph asked, searching her eyes with a concerned look.

Hope nodded, feeling flustered by his proximity. "Jah, I'm fine. I didn't see you either."

Joseph didn't drop his hands, instead he slowly let them trail down her arms before he searched her gaze. "You taught Isaac how to write his name?"

Hope smiled. "He's a fast learner."

"You're a patient teacher, a kind one too." Joseph replied. "We're lucky to have you in our lives."

Hope's heart swelled at his words. His appreciation meant more to her than she had realized it would. His blue eyes held her gaze captive, like it did that night beside the buggy. It was as if the air had thickened, and the rest of the world began to fade away.

There was no doubt left in Hope's mind as she searched Joseph's gaze. She had tried to fool herself for weeks now, but it was no use lying to herself anymore. She didn't just have feelings for Joseph, she was hopelessly and completely in love with him.

Her heart yearned for his love, for his affection. As she searched his blue eyes, she dreamed of a future with him and Isaac.

She caught herself just in time, or she might have revealed her feelings and her dreams to Joseph. She took a swift step back and summoned a tight smile. "I've got to get started on dinner."

Hope turned and headed to the kitchen, needing to put distance between her and Joseph.

The moment she reached the kitchen, she knew there was only one solution to her problem and unwanted feelings for Joseph.

She needed to resign.

THE UNAPPEALING TRUTH

Joseph had picked Beth up a little after noon. Mrs. Schwartz had been kind enough to watch Isaac while he took Beth on their weekly buggy ride.

Usually, Joseph looked forward to seeing Beth all week, but today he didn't feel excited or eager at all. For some reason it felt like another chore he needed to tick off his list of things to do. Instead of cancelling the buggy ride and offending Beth, Joseph had gone ahead and dropped Isaac off before picking Beth up.

They had spent the last fifteen minutes catching up on everything that had happened during the week before the conversation reached a lull. Joseph glanced at Beth from the corner of his eye and found himself still blaming her for not wanting to take care of Isaac on the day of the fire. It had been almost a month ago and he had yet to ask Beth why she had refused.

The more he had thought about it the more it bothered him. He could understand her pouting when he had taken her for ice cream with Isaac without warning her first. But on the day of the fire…

It had been an emergency, one that all the men in the community had been expected to tend to. Surely, she would've understood that?

He glanced at her again and tried to imagine her as his wife, at his dinner table, as a mother figure for Isaac.

Before he could get a clear image in his mind, Beth's words interrupted him.

"Did you hear Eli and Helga got engaged yesterday? They'll be announcing it at Sunday service next week," Beth informed Joseph.

"That's gut news. I'm happy for them." Joseph smiled. He knew Eli well and knew that he had been dreaming of marrying Helga for years.

"Jah me too. There are quite a few weddings coming up this wedding season, I think that's a total of five now," Beth commented, glancing at Joseph.

Joseph nodded. "Jah, quite a year."

They drove in silence for a while, Joseph lost in his own thoughts. Once again Beth's voice interrupted him.

"Joseph, I don't want to be overbearing, but surely you can understand my eagerness for us to become engaged. We've been courting for almost two and a half years now," Beth said the words as if they were an accusation.

"Beth, you know why we haven't gotten engaged yet," Joseph pointed out, meeting her gaze.

Beth sighed. "Jah, your parents, and Isaac. But how long will I have to be second fiddle in your life? You always put Isaac first. What about me?"

Joseph pulled on the reins and brought the buggy to stop. He turned in his seat and met Beth's gaze. "Answer me this, Beth, if I were to ask for your hand today and we were to be married next week, would you raise Isaac as your own? Would you embrace him, and care for him, and teach him? Or will you have better things to do, like you told me the day of the fire?"

Joseph watched as Beth's eyes widened and her mouth opened

then closed as if she rethought her answer. Joseph refused to be angered by her reaction, instead he calmed himself by counting to ten backwards in his mind.

When he reached one, and Beth had yet to answer him, Joseph let out a sigh and shook his head.

"Joseph don't look at me like that. It's not as simple as that. I'm not his guardian," Beth quickly tried to defend herself.

"Nee, you're right. You're not. I am and that means I need to make decisions for my future that include him. There was a time when I knew you were the right woman for me, the woman I wanted to spend my entire life with, but ever since... my situation changed, I don't think that's true anymore. I'm sorry Beth, but it's over between us." As Joseph finished the sentence, he felt as if a mountain had been lifted from his shoulders. A wave of relief washed over him, only now making him realize that Beth had become a burden to him. A burden that wanted him to choose between her and Isaac.

Joseph had finally made that decision and he couldn't be more pleased with it.

"What?" Beth cried out. "You can't just break off our courtship."

Joseph smiled at her sadly. "Beth, admit it. You don't want to become a mother to a five-year-old boy and your feelings for me... they've changed over the last year. You deserve to find someone that will make you happy. You don't deserve to be married only to regret the situation down the line."

Beth sighed and shook her head. "I... although I'm heartbroken, you're right Joseph. I'm not ready to be a mamm to Isaac. I'm sorry."

"At least we had this conversation before we got engaged," Joseph consoled her with half a hug.

They drove back in silence. When Joseph dropped her off, Beth smiled at him a last time before she turned and walked away.

As Joseph drove home, he couldn't help but wonder if Beth had ever truly loved him. If she had, wouldn't she have accepted that Isaac was now part of his life? For the first time he realized the reason he hadn't proposed to her just yet.

Perhaps somewhere deep down he had known that she wasn't the right woman for him. He had hoped that she would change, that she would accept Isaac, but she didn't even deny his presumptions.

Joseph's thoughts turned to Hope. Hope had shown him what Isaac needed. Hope had accepted Isaac with open arms and embraced him, planned or unexpectedly, with love and affection. Would he have known any different if he hadn't hired Hope?

Until now, Joseph had tried his best to ignore the connection he had experienced with Hope, first at her home on the night of the fire, and again a week before. But now that he no longer had a sweetheart, perhaps it was time to explore that connection.

Just perhaps, Hope was the woman he was meant to spend the rest of his life with.

A MOMENT IN TIME

*H*ope had spent the weekend reconsidering her decision to resign.

Even after long walks and numerous prayers, she knew she was making the right decision. She couldn't continue working for a man that she loved but loved another. Just the thought of no longer spending her days with Isaac almost ripped her heart apart, but she knew she didn't have any other choice.

If she were to stay, she would grow to care even more; her sins of coveting growing more as well.

She had stayed up late and written and rewritten her resignation numerous times before she was happy with the result. She had planned on giving it to Joseph when she arrived this morning, but she simply didn't have the heart.

Instead, when she arrived at the Yoder homestead on Monday morning, she realized she needed one more day. One last day to cherish every moment, breathe in Isaac's little boy scent, and memorize Joseph's blue eyes. Hopefully one day would give her enough memories of them to last her a lifetime. Because once she handed Joseph her resignation, Hope had vowed to keep her distance from them in the future.

Joseph needed to focus on his relationship with Beth and Isaac needed to accept that Beth was going to be his new mother-figure.

Just that thought made tears well in Hope's eyes. She blinked them away and focused on Isaac instead. Knowing how much he loved to paint, she had brought along her painting things. After doing chores that morning and cleaning the house, she had packed them a picnic to enjoy on the front lawn while they painted.

Hope tried to absorb every scent, every moment, every word, and still knew it wouldn't be enough to ease the longing she would feel when she said goodbye. She made sure that Isaac didn't pick up on her melancholy. He had already lost his parents and Hope knew losing her would be another tragedy for the little boy. But she still couldn't stay.

If she did, it would be tragedy for her own heart.

When they were done painting, she began to cook supper. Instead of the usual stew or pasta she cooked for them on Mondays, she went through the effort of cooking a ham with vegetables and mashed potatoes.

Isaac was drawing at the table, quietly entertaining himself as Hope worked. When she had finished mashing the potatoes, Isaac stood up to see what was in the pot.

"Squashed 'tatoes?" Isaac asked hopefully.

Hope laughed. "Jah, squashed potatoes. Your favorite."

"Hmmm yum." Isaac demonstrated by licking his lips.

"All Hope's food is yum," Joseph said, surprising her by returning early from the fields.

This hadn't been part of her plan. She had wanted to finish up for the day and then wait for Joseph on the porch where she would talk to him in private. "Denke," she replied quietly.

She didn't dare meet his gaze, afraid of drowning in his eyes. "You're done early?"

"Jah, thought I'd spend some time with my favorite people." Joseph scooped Isaac up and tossed him over his shoulder.

Isaac's giggles filled the kitchen, making Hope's tummy twist with emotion.

Was she one of his favorite people? She quickly pushed the thought aside, he didn't mean her, he meant Isaac, she reminded herself.

For a moment, Hope just stood there and watched them. She took in the moment and knew that she was going to miss them as if they had once belonged to her.

She knew that fate had dealt both Isaac and Joseph a foul hand by taking their parents, but Hope couldn't help but wonder if Joseph and Isaac knew how lucky they were to have each other. It was as if losing their parents had brought them closer than they would've ever been otherwise.

Joseph turned and set Isaac down before meeting her gaze with a questioning look. "Are you alright, Hope?"

Hope quickly summoned a smile. "Jah, I'm fine. I must finish slicing the ham then I'll be on my way."

"There's no rush," Joseph insisted with a warm smile. "You're welcome to stay for dinner, we'd love to have you."

Hope quickly shook her head. "I have other plans." She turned away from Joseph, praying for courage to do what she had to do.

A short while later she slid the sliced ham back into the now cold oven before she collected her purse from the pantry. Joseph and Isaac were sitting out on the porch. Joseph was reading to Isaac from the bible, a verse that Hope had loved as a child.

Psalm 100:3. *"Know that the Lord is God. It is he who made us, and we are his; we are his people, the sheep of his pasture."*

"But I'm not a sheep?" Isaac asked with a frown.

Joseph laughed, unaware of Hope's presence. "Nee, we're not sheep. But what that means is that Gott cares for us and protects us, like a shepherd does for his sheep."

Hope's heart felt crushed beneath the overwhelming

emotions that flooded her. "I uhm," she cleared her throat of the tears just waiting to fall. "I'm ready to leave."

"Denke for dinner," Joseph said, turning to her with a smile.

"Did you know we're *like* sheep?" Isaac asked with a frown.

Hope laughed. "Jah, Gott's sheep. Kumm, give me a hug before I go."

Isaac hopped off Joseph's lap and rushed into Hope's waiting arms. She hugged him tightly before letting him go. "Be gut."

"I will," Isaac nodded with a grin.

Hope moved towards Joseph and pulled the letter out of her purse. "Please read this when I'm gone."

Joseph frowned as he accepted the envelope. "What's this?"

"Denke for everything." Hope didn't waste another second; she knew her tears were imminent. She turned and began to walk faster than she ever had before. She managed to bite back the tears until she was at least a hundred yards from the homestead.

When they finally spilled over her cheeks, Hope knew they wouldn't stop for quite some time. She hadn't just lost her job; she had also lost the man she had come to love. The man she had dreamed of sharing a future with.

And the boy she loved like a son.

HOPE-LESS

Joseph could tell something was very wrong by the way Hope had said goodbye. He glanced at the letter on the table and feared what would be inside.

"Can we eat now, I'm starving?" Isaac asked beside him.

Joseph looked at the array of food on the table and realized he had no appetite at all. "Of course."

Joseph picked at his food, more pushing it around the plate than eating it. By the time Isaac's plate was empty it was bath time.

As most evenings, one thing led to another, and Isaac's babbling didn't stop until he finally put him down for the night. Joseph told him a story, although his mind kept returning to the letter on the kitchen table.

When he finally left Isaac's room, Joseph was even more afraid of the contents of the letter than he had been before. It was as if a dark cloud had settled over his shoulders, warning him that whatever was in that letter wasn't something he wanted to hear.

Knowing he couldn't delay reading it forever, he finally made himself a cup of coffee before he headed to the porch. The flower baskets that had been empty since his parents had passed away, now boasted beautiful impatiens spilling over in full bloom. It was just another thing Joseph hadn't asked Hope to do, but which she had done on her own.

Small things that made his house feel like a home again, he thought as he sat down on the rocking chair.

He opened the letter and began to read.

Dear Joseph

I want to thank you for giving me the privilege of caring for Isaac these last few months.

Unfortunately, I won't be able to continue with my services as Isaac's nanny. I hope you understand that I didn't make this decision lightly. Please do not ask me to reconsider this decision. I hope you can respect it.

I wish both you and Isaac all the blessings our merciful Gott can afford you.

Regards,

Hope

Joseph's forehead creased with heavy frown even as that same heaviness settled over his heart. The thought of not seeing Hope every day, not having her laughter and her warmth in his house, made him feel bereft.

A heavy sigh escaped him realizing that Isaac was going to feel her absence even more. Isaac had come to love Hope, there wasn't a single doubt in Joseph's mind about that. When the two of them were together they had a bond, a connection that was special. It was exactly what Isaac had needed, and now it was gone.

Joseph shook his head, baffled at why Hope would resign so suddenly. They hadn't argued or even had a difference of opinion. Her resignation had come as unexpectedly as snow in the height of summer. It just didn't make any sense.

What was more disheartening was now that Beth was no longer in Joseph's life, he had looked forward to exploring the connection he had felt with Hope. He had no idea where it would lead, but it had felt strong enough that Joseph had been eager to explore it.

Joseph glanced down at her words and realized that although Hope had been Isaac's nanny, she had become much more than that to both him and his brother.

When he'd broken up with Beth, he had felt a sort of relief wash over him, but now…

This wasn't relief.

It was heartbreak.

His heart felt as if it was being torn into a million pieces by her words. It felt as if he had just lost a friend, a loved one…

The realization made his breath catch. He had been curious about the connection he had with Hope, but he had never thought it could be love. The more he thought about it, the more he realized that was what he felt for Hope.

His feelings for her came unexpectedly, without him even realizing it. He had been so focused on how wonderful she was to Isaac, that he hadn't for a moment stopped to accept that she had been just as wonderful to him.

All the meals, the chores, the small gestures she had done to make their house a home again, had made him realize that since his parents had passed away, he had simply gone through every day to make it to the next.

But with Hope, both he and Isaac had begun to look forward to the next day again. It wasn't just her food, or the way she was with Isaac, it was everything about her.

She was kind beyond comparison to anyone he'd ever met before. She was generous, and friendly, and considerate, and most of all she was loving and affectionate. Joseph had never realized how important those characteristics were until he witnessed his brother blossom under her care.

Joseph looked up at the stars and wished he knew what to do next. She hadn't given her reasons for resigning, but Joseph could understand from her letter that it had been a difficult decision for her. Perhaps it was because her mother needed her at home, or perhaps she had found a better position elsewhere.

She made it clear that he shouldn't contact her about reconsidering, which left him at loss. A stab of pain shot through his heart, realizing he had to break the news to his brother in the morning. It was hard enough for Joseph to lose Hope, but for his brother…

This loss would be just another loss that his brother had to face. Joseph felt tears burn his eyes. He wanted to protect his brother, but he couldn't protect him from this.

Needing guidance, advice, or simply consolation, Joseph searched the sky before he began to pray.

"Gott please help me understand what I need to do next. I broke up with Beth because I knew she wasn't the right person for Isaac and me to share our home with. Now I am left without a sweetheart and Isaac no longer has the nanny he had come to love.

The nanny I had come to love.

Lord, I'm not sure I can deal with this loss. It hurts, Lord, more than I ever expected it would. I beg of you, give me strength. Give me strength and wisdom to help Isaac through this...

I also want to ask you to protect and bless Hope. She is so deserving of your blessings, Lord. Her kindness and love have truly brought me and Isaac back to life after losing our parents. Please Gott, I beg this of you.

Amen."

JOSEPH SAT on the porch for a while longer, wondering what he was going to do. It would be impossible to find childcare within a few days and he still believed the daycare center wasn't an option.

Finally, he gave up and headed to bed. When he rested his head on the pillow, he hoped that with a new day would come new strength and new hope.

Because right now, he felt hopeless.

Literally Hope-less.

BEREFT WITHOUT HOPE

ope knew she had made the right decision to resign.

She couldn't keep working for a man she dreamed of calling her husband and a child she hoped to become a mother to. Every day she stayed would've broken her heart more than leaving.

But leaving had very nearly crushed her heart.

She hadn't revealed her reasons to her family, or to Joseph for that matter. It was bad enough that she was in love with a man that was about to become engaged. No one else needed to know of her feelings.

Feelings that refused to go away.

Instead, she had told her parents that Joseph had relieved her of her services. She knew her parents had come to rely on the money, and the guilt haunted her every day. Hope had vowed to herself that she would find another job, she would contribute to her family again. But for now, she would stay home and nurse her wounded heart.

Spending every minute of every day thinking about Joseph and Isaac.

She thought of them when she woke up, wondering what

their plans would be for the day. Over breakfast she wondered if Isaac would join Joseph in the fields or if Joseph would stay home. When lunch time rolled around, she wondered what they would have for lunch.

She worried about the house that wasn't being cleaned, about the plants that weren't being watered, and about Isaac who wouldn't have his daily lesson.

But most of all she worried if she would ever be able to move on with her life.

Joseph and Isaac had become such a big part of her life, that not even her big family could seem to fill the chasm leaving them had caused.

Her mother hadn't asked her outright, but Hope knew her mother suspected something was wrong. Instead of putting Hope to work like she would've done in the past, she gave Hope space to keep herself busy. Whether it be with laundry, gardening, or simply scrubbing the floors until they gleamed, her mother didn't ask any questions.

Hope had never been more grateful for her mother's intuitiveness.

As if sensing Hope needed some time alone, her mother had gone into town to do the weekly marketing with all her siblings. Only Peter had stayed behind to help his father in the fields.

It had been a week since she'd seen Joseph and Isaac. There hadn't even been a church service yesterday where she could've at least seen if they were doing well without her.

Once her mother had left with the buggy, Hope decided that she would use the time alone to work through her feelings of loss. Hopefully when nightfall came, she would have a plan about moving on with her life.

Although she couldn't fathom how she would find a solution to her problem, since not even prayer had helped thus far.

Needing to busy her hands, Hope headed into the hayloft and searched through all the old furniture and items stored there, for something to do. She finally found an old chest that had been stowed there by generations of Maas that had lived there before her.

With Peter's help she managed to get it down from the hayloft. Determined to return it to its former glory, Hope believed that if she restored a hope chest for herself, perhaps it would renew her hope for the future.

First, she began by scrubbing it down with sugar soap. It was layered with years of dirt and grime. She dragged it into the yard to dry in the sun. The wood was stained and scarred in numerous places she observed once it was dry. She had hoped to sand it down and give it a good layer of oil to restore the wood, but assessing the wood, that wouldn't work.

Instead, the chest needed a coat of paint to restore it back to life. Just like Hope needed a new dream to bring her back to life.

A dream that didn't include Joseph and Isaac.

A heavy sigh escaped her when she imagined herself hearing Isaac's voice. Hope closed her eyes and tried to shake the sound from her mind. She couldn't keep living in the past, she needed to move on.

"Hope!"

When she heard his voice again, Hope turned towards the direction it came from.

She hadn't been reliving a memory, Isaac was jumping out of the buggy as he began to run towards her. Hope's eyes welled with tears of joy when he slammed into her legs and held on tight.

Hope didn't know why he was there, all she cared about was holding him in her arms again. She scooped him up and held him close, drawing in the scent of little boy and sunshine. "Hullo."

Isaac clasped his arms around her neck so tightly he was almost suffocating her, but Hope didn't dare ask him to let go.

"Isaac, you're crushing her," Joseph's voice came from a few feet away.

Hope opened her eyes, and her heart skipped a beat at the sight of Joseph. "Joseph?"

She put Isaac down and frowned at the man she had come to love.

"Hullo Hope. I'm so sorry for intruding like this, but I really don't have any other choice. A few men are on their way to my farm to help me burn firebreaks against the main road. If I had any other option, I wouldn't have bothered you, but I don't. It simply isn't safe for Isaac to be there while we're doing the burns. Can you…"

Hope didn't even wait for him to ask. "Jah, I'll watch him."

"Are you sure? I know you said…" Joseph trailed off, careful of what he said in front of Isaac.

"I'd love to watch him," Hope insisted. "He can help me restore this old chest."

Joseph held her gaze for a moment and Hope felt love spread through her. She had missed him terribly, but she couldn't tell him that. He wasn't hers… he belonged to Beth.

A few moments later Joseph nodded before he headed to his buggy and drove away.

Hope led Isaac to the chest and swallowed back the tears that had welled in her eyes. She wouldn't cry, not today. Not when she had a few hours to spend with her favorite child in the whole world. "Have you ever painted a chest before?"

"Nee," Isaac shook his head. "Isn't it just like painting on paper?"

Hope chuckled. "It's a little different. For example, we only use one color of paint. And we need to use sandpaper on the chest first."

Isaac nodded eagerly. "What can I do?"

Hope scooped him up in another tight hug. "First, you can give me another squeeze."

Isaac did just that.

The next few hours flew by as Hope and Isaac worked on the

chest. When her mother returned with her other siblings, Daniel and Rose joined in on the effort. Hope spent more time making sure the paint landed on the chest and not on their clothes, but it felt wonderful to hear Isaac's laughter and to have him close.

While the first layer of paint was left to dry in the sun, Hope led the children into the kitchen where she treated them to cookies and cool drinks.

"If you love that child so much, why did Joseph ask you to leave?" Ruth asked her daughter with a cocked brow.

Hope sighed as she met her mother's gaze. "He didn't ask me to leave, Mamm."

"Louisa, watch the young ones, your schweschder and I need to talk," Ruth said to second eldest daughter before she led Hope towards her bedroom. Once the door was closed behind them, she turned to Hope with a questioning look. "I've watch you mope around this yard for a week, as if you lost a loved one. I didn't ask, thinking that when you were ready, you'd talk to me. Now I'm asking, what's going on, Hope?"

Hope felt a tear slip over her cheek. "Ach, it's such a ferhoodled mess, Mamm, I don't even know where to begin."

"At the beginning," Ruth suggested.

Hope sat down on the bed and let out a heavy sigh before she began to tell her mother everything. She told her mother about how her feelings for Joseph had developed and how she had prayed for Gott to take them away. She explained about Beth and the upcoming engagement and continued to explain about how she had come to care for Isaac.

When she explained about resigning, her mother reached for her hand.

"I'm so sorry, dochder. I had no idea. I knew you cared for Isaac, but I didn't realize you had feelings for Joseph..."

"It's not right, Mamm, he has a sweetheart. I just couldn't stay there, knowing that it was only a matter of time before Beth would be his frau and a new mamm to Isaac." Hope sniffed and shook her head. "But I miss them, Mamm, I miss them terribly."

Her mother pulled her lose and held her while she wept. When the sobs finally subsided, her mother pulled back and met her gaze. "You did the right thing dochder. Just trust in the Lord, he will guide you through this towards your future happiness."

"I pray for that, Mamm, every day." Hope smiled weakly.

"Kumm, you don't know how much longer you have him for, make the best of it," Ruth encouraged, standing up.

Hope nodded. "Jah, I'm going to do just that."

Before Hope could leave the room, her mother reached for her arm and turned her to face her. "Just remember, Hope, that sometimes we don't understand our own hearts, our own emotions, but Gott does. Perhaps you feel this way for a reason, a reason that is yet to be revealed to you? Joseph is a gut mann, have you considered he might feel the same way?"

Hope shook her head. "If he felt something for me, Mamm, why would he be courting Beth?"

Her mother shrugged. "Sometimes things aren't as they appear."

TALKS BY THE TREE LINE

It was late afternoon by the time they had finished with the firebreaks. Joseph felt much more at ease knowing that if a fire were to start next to the highway, he had a small margin of protection before the fire would reach his crops.

Joseph pulled into the Maas homestead and felt his stomach coil like a tight spring at the thought of seeing Hope again. When he'd seen her this morning, it had felt as if the sun had shone on him for the first time in a week.

The way she had welcomed Isaac, holding him as if her whole world revolved around him, he hadn't expected anything less. He knew he couldn't make a habit of asking her to help with Isaac, but hopefully today would've been good for Isaac as well. Isaac hadn't been himself ever since Joseph explained that Hope wouldn't be returning.

As he climbed out of his buggy, he could hear the laughter of children and Hope coming from around the barn. Joseph followed the sound and found them playing a game of catch. Isaac was beaming and Hope was laughing in that easy way she did when he wasn't around. Joseph's heart clenched in his chest, wishing he knew why she had resigned.

He hadn't pressed for her an explanation, he had honored her wishes, but looking at her now, he knew he couldn't just let her go. Before he left today, he needed to know why she had resigned, especially if she loved spending time with Isaac so much.

She spotted him and stopped running the moment their eyes met. Joseph moved towards her, children running through and around them, continuing the game. "Can we talk?"

Her eyes widened, almost with fear. "Joseph, I…"

"I'll watch the kinner. You go on," Ruth answered before Hope could think of an excuse.

Joseph shot a grateful look at Ruth before he led Hope away from the children. They walked into the fields towards a tree line in the distance. The further they could walk, the more time he could have with her, Joseph reasoned.

Once they reached the tree line, he turned to her with his heart on his sleeve. "We've missed you, Hope."

Her eyes widened but she didn't say word.

Joseph shook his head and reached for her hand. "Why did you resign? I must know, Hope. Is it something I said, something I did? I know you love Isaac, so it must have been because of me."

Hope sighed and shook her head. "Joseph, please don't do this."

"Do what, ask for honesty?" Joseph pushed a little further. "Did you at least miss us?"

Hope held his gaze and narrowed her eyes. "You said you missed me, are you speaking on behalf of yourself or Isaac?"

"Both of us. I missed your laughter, your cooking, your company… all of it," Joseph explained, trying to be clear that he cared about her.

"That's why I resigned," Hope finally admitted. "You are about to be engaged to Beth, Joseph."

Joseph frowned as he read between the lines. "Hope, do you have feelings for me?"

Hope's face flushed bright red. She quickly looked away, but it was too late, Joseph had already read the answer in her eyes.

He reached for her chin and turned her head to meet his gaze. "Hope, I broke off everything with Beth two days before you resigned. There is no upcoming engagement or wedding."

Hope's eyes widened with surprise. "What? Why?"

Joseph shrugged. "Because I realized that she wasn't the person I wanted to spend the rest of my life with. Because she couldn't accept that Isaac was part of my life. Because... because she simply wasn't you. I knew we had a connection, but I wasn't sure what it was or what to do. I thought that I could explore it after I broke up with Beth, but then you left. It was only when you left that I realized that we had more than just a connection..."

Hope's eyes narrowed. "What are you saying, Joseph?"

Joseph smiled lovingly into Hope's gaze. "I might have been courting Beth, but without realizing it, I fell in love with you, Hope. Do feel the same, is that why you resigned?"

Hope's breath caught, surprised, and flustered by his words. "I... I never wanted to have feelings for you Joseph, it just happened. I was supposed to be Isaac's nanny but before I realized it, I began to dream of sharing a future with both of you. I fell in love with both of you. I couldn't stay... knowing that you loved Beth."

Joseph wrapped his arms around her and held her close. Nothing in the world had ever felt righter than having Hope Maas in his arms. It was as if his heart became whole and his dreams were renewed, knowing that Hope could be his.

He had delayed asking Beth for her hand in marriage for more than two years, needing to find certainty in his heart. But as he stepped back and searched Hope's gaze, Joseph found all the certainty he never had with Beth. He could see his future in her gaze, he could see the love she had for him and the love she had for Isaac.

Joseph didn't even hesitate. He went down on one knee and looked up at Hope as he held her hand. "Hope, I could ask you on a buggy ride and I could ask for your permission to court you, but I don't want to waste another minute. You made our house a home, you brought life back into our grief and you won over our hearts with your kindness and love. Please do me the honor of accepting my hand in marriage. Be my frau, be a mamm to Isaac, and build a familye and a life with me."

"Joseph… but we haven't even been on a buggy ride?" Hope asked, wide-eyed with shock.

Joseph shrugged. "We've spent more time getting to know each other over the last few months than any number of buggy rides could ever achieve. I love you Hope, and I think you love me. That's all that matters."

Hope hesitated for a moment before her mouth curved into a smile. "Jah, I'll marry you."

Joseph laughed as he stood up and drew her into his arms. Hope's sweet voice whispered into his ear. "I've missed you so much…"

Joseph stood back and met her gaze. "Keeping our feelings from each other nearly cost us our future. Let's promise to never keep anything from each other again."

Hope nodded. "Agreed."

EPILOGUE

Parents and children were gathered outside the schoolhouse. Hope couldn't help but feel a little anxious about today. She still couldn't believe that it had been two years since she and Joseph had admitted their feelings to each other.

That day had been followed by a whirlwind of planning with the wedding and Hope's move to the Yoder homestead. The wedding had been a simple affair with only their closest and dearest in attendance.

Knowing how much her family had depended on her income, Joseph had graciously opened a bank account for her parents and deposited a monthly stipend into it, to ease their financial burdens.

If Hope had been anxious about moving to the Yoder homestead, she had soon realized her worries had been for naught. She fell into the routine she had upheld with Isaac and quickly adjusted to being a wife. Within a matter of months, all of Hope's dreams had been realized.

Ever since that day, she still thanked the Lord every day for blessing her so generously.

The school bell rang, and Hope's breath caught when Isaac raced towards the door. "I'll see you later."

"Be gut and mind the teacher," Joseph warned.

"I will," Isaac answered with a toothless grin. He had lost his first baby tooth just the week before.

Isaac turned to Hope and gave her a tight hug before he stepped back. "Don't miss me too much."

Hope smiled, biting back the emotions that overwhelmed her.

She watched Isaac join his fellow first graders as they rushed into the schoolhouse.

"He's going to be just fine," Joseph said wrapping his arm around Hope's shoulders.

Hope knew that Joseph was right, but that didn't make her cry any less. She glanced back over her shoulder at the one room schoolhouse and felt her heart break all over again. "I can't believe he's seven already," Hope sniffed.

Joseph chuckled. "They tend to grow up. I thought you'd be relieved now that he's starting the first grade."

Hope turned to Joseph with horrified expression. "Why would you think that? I love having Isaac around. I'm going to miss him."

"It's just a few hours a day, Hope," Joseph said, giving his wife half a hug. "You've prepared him better than any other first grader he's starting with. He's going to make friends and learn new things and you'll have the mornings free to spend with Grace."

Hope nodded as she smiled down at her nine-month-old daughter in the stroller she was pushing. "I know it's gut for Isaac, it's just an emotional day for a..."

"Mother." Joseph finished for her. "I won't ever take offense of you thinking of Isaac as your own. He's blessed to have you. Both of us are blessed to have you. I wanted to ask you something. He wants to know if he can call you mamm?"

Hope's eyes widened. She had never expected Isaac to call her mamm, after all, he was her husband's brother. Actually, he was her brother-in-law, not her son. But in her heart, he felt like her son. "If he wants, and you approve... I would love that," Hope admitted.

Joseph nodded. "Then it's settled." He glanced at Grace in the stroller and chuckled softly.

"What's so funny?" Hope asked with a smile, feeling a little better. She knew that going to the first grade was exciting for Isaac, she also knew it was necessary. But just like with any other mother, big milestones reminded you that they wouldn't rely on you forever.

"Us," Joseph admitted. "I still can't believe that I once thought that Beth was the right frau for me. And you keeping your feelings from me... If I hadn't decided to burn firebreaks that day, I might have never confronted you about your resignation."

Hope nodded. She had thought about that numerous times in the two years since they were married. "I was ashamed of my feelings; you were courting Beth after all."

"And now she's happily married to Eli Brahmer. Everything happens for a reason and Gott is the reason behind everything."

"He is," Hope agreed. She turned to her husband with a smile of pride and love. "Your parents would've been so proud of you Joseph. You've become a wunderbaar daed to him."

Joseph swallowed, clearly deeply affected by her words. "Denke, that means a lot to me."

Hope nodded. "I know. You always say that I'm the heart and soul of our home, but did you know that you are the support beams? You're always there, always ready to help, always willing to take care of us, regardless of what you need to do on the farm."

"That's what a mann is supposed to do. I tend the farm to care for my familye, but without my familye the farm won't matter and that's why you always come first," Joseph insisted.

Hope's heart swelled with love. "What are your plans for the day?"

"Today?" Joseph asked with a thoughtful look. "Today I plan on spending the morning with my frau and my dochder, and this afternoon I'm going to collect Isaac from school and take him for an ice cream. I think he deserves an ice cream on his first day of school?"

Hope's heart swelled at her husband's thoughtfulness. It was hard to remember a time when she found Joseph imposing. Now she knew him to be kind, generous, and loving. Isaac was blessed to have him as a brother and a father figure, just like their baby girl was blessed to be his daughter.

There had been a time when she had thought Gott wasn't hearing her prayers, but she knew now that Gott had heard her prayers all along.

Instead of doing what she asked of him, he patiently took the reins of her life and led her towards the future he had planned for her.

A future with a beautiful familye.

*** The End ***

THANK you kindly for choosing to read my book. I sincerely hope you enjoyed it. All my Amish Romances are wholesome stories suitable for all to enjoy.

If you could be so kind to leave a review on Amazon, I would appreciate it.